MW01254729

Bewitching Blend

A Paramour Bay Mystery
Book Two

KENNEDY LAYNE

BEWITCHING BLEND

Copyright © 2018 by Kennedy Layne
Print Edition

eBook ISBN: 978-1-943420-64-3
Print ISBN: 978-1-943420-65-0

Cover Designer: Sweet 'N Spicy Designs

ALL RIGHTS RESERVED: The unauthorized reproduction or distribution of this copyrighted work is illegal. Criminal copyright infringement is investigated by the FBI and is punishable by up to 5 years in federal prison and a fine of $250,000.

All characters and events in this book are fictitious. Any resemblance to actual persons living or dead is strictly coincidental.

DEDICATION

Jeffrey—You bewitched me with that very first email...I love you!

Cole—May your college journey be bewitching in every way!

Welcome back to Paramour Bay as USA Today Bestselling Author Kennedy Layne continues her cozy paranormal mystery series that will have you brewing up a cup of tea well past midnight...

It's been two months since Raven Marigold discovered she was a witch, and she is handling her situation with grace. Well, if you discount the fact that she caught her blouse on fire and made her cat's tail go numb for four hours. The bottom line is that Raven is succeeding in her pursuit of this new mystical life she's been given.

Someone must have missed that memo, though. Raven finds herself smack dab in the middle of another murder investigation. Every piece of evidence points to the town treasurer as being the guilty party, but she isn't so sure the case is that cut and dried.

It is then that Raven gets the brilliant idea of using a bit of witchcraft to help out the handsome, young sheriff. After all, what could go wrong with a bewitching blend, an enchanted spell book, and a haunted inn on the edge of town?

Chapter One

"CAN YOU BELIEVE that the town of Paramour Bay is being audited?"

I managed to keep my head down as I packaged the special blend of tea leaves with the added ingredients that were essential to ease Wilma Dawson's cold symptoms. She'd been sneezing into her delicate lace embroidered hanky almost nonstop since she'd entered the shop, and I had no doubt that her best friend standing beside her would be purchasing the special concoction before week's end.

Elsie and Wilma's endearing propensity for gossip had been keeping me in the know this past month, for which I was remarkably grateful in spite of their bias. Being a newcomer had its own limitations, but the fact that they were both in their mid-seventies didn't escape me. Their skewed view of certain matters didn't surprise me at all.

I really needed to get out more.

What's wrong with Ted?

I ignored the irritating, scratchy voice floating through my head reminding me of the odd man who lived on my property on the edge of town. Ted had technically come with the house. That's quite a long story, so I'll leave that for later.

Unfortunately, my best friend lived over two very long hours away by train in New York City. I saw Heidi maybe twice a month on weekends, but it wasn't nearly enough. I missed our wine nights during the work week, our coffee sprees on Saturday mornings, and the binging of enthralling television shows that we'd take part in on rainy Sunday afternoons.

Those were the days...

"I bet Mayor Sanders is fit to be tied. He doesn't much care for the county or the state poking their bent noses into our small-town business. You know how he likes to coddle his ego." Elsie barely took a breather between words as she reached into her handbag and pulled out another hanky, this one dry. "Here. You know, I don't think it was such a good idea for us to keep our hair appointments today. You should be home and resting in bed with your constitution all fouled up the way it is."

"But then we wouldn't have found out that Gillian Reilly has gone and gotten herself pregnant with twins," Wilma responded in a rather nasally tone. She delicately wiped her nose before slipping the fancy cotton cloth up her sleeve. "She must be so elated. Gillian and her husband have been trying for quite a few months now."

"Isn't it just the best news? Although, I still can't believe that Larry summoned the courage to ask Mindy Walsh out for dinner this weekend," Elsie added on, apparently conceding Wilma's point about keeping their weekly visit to the salon. They both shook their heads in commiseration and spoke in unison. "Poor, poor Abbie."

I couldn't help but smile, though not at the fact that Abbie's ex-husband had finally asked another woman out on a date. It was just that these two ladies never failed to entertain me with their reactions to the events in other people's mundane lives.

It was rather amusing to hear their opinions.

One would think that Elsie and Wilma never had time to

stop and watch television, but I'd been on the receiving end of being explained the comings and goings of shady characters on various soap operas.

I was fully convinced that Paramour Bay topped the nefarious plots on any fictional show on TV.

I wouldn't say that. Have you seen the last season of "The Walking Dead"? You know, we do have access to Netflix out here in the sticks.

You must be wondering about the voice I keep hearing inside my head. For that matter, you must be wondering who I am and how I've come to be a resident of Paramour Bay. Well, let me quickly catch you up.

My name is Raven Lattice Marigold, and I'm a witch of sorts.

Yes, you heard that right. It's okay if you need to take a minute to absorb such astounding news. It took me more than a few myself. I still have moments of doubt regarding my own sanity.

But the truth is, I'm an actual bona fide witch...a beginner, really. My stomach still gets those odd butterfly sensations every time I think about my evolving gift. My mother kept referring to it as the family curse, but my grandmother managed to lure me here to Paramour Bay for a reason—to discover my true calling.

You see, I was your average everyday woman living in New York City just trying to get by when I received a phone call that my Nan had passed away. We'd been estranged for years due to my mother, so don't get too choked up. I didn't realize it at the time, but my mother wanted no part of our family legacy and had endeavored to keep me in the dark about all of it. Had I known, it would have made this transition a lot easier for all of us.

You can imagine the shock I went through in discovering the dark family secret—the Marigolds were honest to goodness, dyed in the wool, real witches.

Anyway, a long story short, Nan ended up leaving me her quaint little tea shop called *Tea, Leaves, & Eves* in the very small town of Paramour Bay, Connecticut. There were some stipulations contained in her last wishes, of course, but we'll get into those provisions later.

Right now, the most important thing you should know is that Nan used a bit of not-so-white magic—for a good reason, I might add—to keep her familiar alive so that I had someone to clue me in on the rites and practices of my birthright. It probably wasn't one of her best incantations in hindsight, but that's where Leo enters the picture.

Mr. Leo to you.

I continued to ignore him, as usual.

Elsie and Wilma couldn't hear Leo, though they could see the ruffian as he lounged in the warm rays of the morning sun shining through the large display window at the front of the shop. What little heat the sunshine provided was rather deceiving, seeing as it was the first week of December in Connecticut. Flurries were expected in the forecast later today, which meant Leo would probably remain in that exact same spot until the clouds moved in and took away his heat source.

Unfortunately, there *was* a slight problem with Leo's rather tragic appearance. My explanation that he was a rescue cat who'd been in a dreadful accident seemed to hold with the townsfolk, though.

Just say it. I resemble Frankenstein's pet cat.

It was true, but I usually tried to keep my opinions to myself. It wasn't easy, because he could read all of my thoughts.

Nevertheless, Leo tended to be overly sarcastic. It was easy to forget he had feelings, but he certainly was not a powerful witch's familiar that I wanted on my bad side. I shuddered to think of the level to which he'd stoop in order to get his point across.

Nevertheless, I can sum up Leo's appearance in one word—horrific.

I'm being serious.

His whiskers were bent at every odd angle imaginable, his orange and black fur had tufts sticking out everywhere, his tail resembled a wire hanger bent at random ninety-degree angles, and his left eye was noticeably larger than his right. Truthfully, it was a bit disconcerting to look directly at him. It also didn't help that he was overweight and his legs were rather short, similar to an Oompa Loompa household cat.

You should have seen me in my glory days.

"Did Mindy say yes to Larry's dinner proposal?" I asked, giving the two women my attention as I rung up Wilma's sale on my new cash register. I'd even gotten one of those credit card machines to make purchases easier for my customers, though it hadn't been used in the few days the small device had been sitting on the counter since all of my customers paid in cash. They'd done so for years with my Nan. "I think it's good for Larry to move on after his divorce. And Mindy is an absolute sweetheart."

Still on the subject of my looks, have you seen the latest style? I'll have you know that long hair and scruffy beards are back in. I'm no different than those GQ models with a five o'clock shadow.

"We'd heard from a friend that you and Mindy had lunch together the other day," Elsie said with a sparkle in her eyes before sidling up to the counter. She didn't seem to care that

Wilma was digging in her sleeve for the hanky she'd stored up there just ten seconds ago. "It's good to see you making friends, my dear."

I could just imagine what the residents of Paramour Bay thought of me after my initial arrival. It had been like falling through a trap door.

Did I mention that I found a dead body in the back of my shop?

I did, and it had come right on the heels of my arrival. Of course, it had caused all kinds of excitement seeing as the last murder to have taken place in this tiny town was over fifty-three years ago.

Let's just hope I hadn't started a trend, because I'm relatively sure the townsfolk would run me out of town on a rail. I shuddered to think what these good citizens would do if they discovered I was actually a witch.

I would go into more detail about the murder investigation, but Wilma was staring out the display window while repeatedly shoving her elbow into Elsie's side. I didn't even have to follow their stares to know that Sheriff Liam Drake was leaving the station to walk next door to the diner for lunch.

My heart fluttered when I saw that he glanced my way.

"Here you go, Wilma."

I set the brown paper bag of tea leaves that I'd sealed with one of the shop's gold re-sealable stickers on the counter rather abruptly, along with her receipt. If they wanted more gossip to spread around town, they'd have to find it elsewhere today. The last thing I needed was to be fodder for the gossip mill after my name had finally managed to fade from the spotlight.

Besides, there was absolutely nothing going on between me and the good sheriff of Paramour Bay.

If you think that's true, I'm not so sure this witch thing is going to work out for you.

I had to bite my tongue so that I didn't yell at Leo for trying to instigate me into saying something about Liam in front of Elsie and Wilma. An outburst of any kind would certainly have them wagging their tongues for days to come. The town seemed to hang on their every word.

"I hope you feel better, Wilma," I conveyed sincerely before grabbing the folder I'd put together last night for my upcoming meeting. It was my first official sales appointment since I'd taken over the tea shop. I have to admit that I'm a tad bit nervous. "I'm going to close up the shop for around thirty minutes while I walk over to the Paramour Bay Inn. Gertie wants to place her annual order for the guests, and I've put together a list that I think will give the visitors to our small town a variety of choices to drink during their stays."

Their shared glance of unease had the hairs on the back of my neck standing to attention.

"What?" My gaze bounced from Elsie to Wilma and then back to Elsie. She was more likely to spill details than her friend. "What's wrong? Tell me straight away."

"We heard that those auditors booked five rooms at the inn," Elsie finally shared, slipping the strap of her purse over her shoulder while Wilma took her bag off the counter. I wasn't sure I'd heard her right, because I was expecting them to tell me that Gertie had decided to go outside of Paramour Bay to purchase her tea. That would have been catastrophic. "You know what that means, don't you?"

"That the auditors needed a place to stay?" I asked, truly lost in this conversation.

You aren't the only one. These two give me a headache.

Leo stretched his legs when one of those snow clouds I talked about earlier must have floated by and cloaked the warm rays of sunshine. He even yawned, though Elsie and Wilma had no idea that he'd done so on purpose to show his level of boredom.

How you listen to these two go on and on about their idea of conspiracies is beyond me. We have more important things to do, anyway, now that we've found Rosemary's spell book.

I guess now would be a good time for me to admit that the tea blend I'd put together for Wilma's cold had a magical spell attached to the leaves, along with the sundry material components I'd added to the blend. Don't get me wrong, the antioxidants of the tea were extremely healthy. I'd also added ginger root, lemongrass, orange peel, and other ingredients to name a few to aid in equalizing the body's balance.

You're leaving out the health invocation I taught you last week. You know, the one you didn't manage to mess up?

What Leo didn't mention was that I almost hadn't learned any spells at all, thanks to the protection wards that my Nan placed on the spell book before she died.

Remember the body I mentioned earlier? The one I'd found in the storage room of the tea shop on my first day?

Well, that man had actually been a wizard from a competing family who'd been trying to steal my grandmother's spells for ages. She must have known that was a possibility, so she'd bound the special book with several wards that protected the family incantations that had been handed down through the generations.

I'm getting off topic, though.

Thankfully, Wilma decided to say something that garnered my attention.

"Of course, the auditors needed a place to stay, but Elsie was referring to the fact that there are five of them." Wilma leaned over the counter as she lowered her voice. I pulled back slightly, not wanting to catch her cold. The last thing I needed was to get sick before the holiday season kicked off. "Two men and three women are looking into the town's finances. You should really try to find out why they're here when you go over to the inn this afternoon."

Elsie nodded her head, as if encouraging me to do Wilma's bidding.

"Aren't they here to audit the town's finances?" I must have missed something earlier in the chinwag train, because an audit was just an audit, right? Why were these two acting like it was the end of the known world? "I'm sure this is a very common practice."

"That's not what we heard," Elsie shared as she stole a glance toward the exit.

Were they expecting the auditors to waltz in here and have them slapped in irons for gossiping about them?

We could only hope.

Leo wasn't helping my cause, which was to close up the shop for thirty minutes while I walked down to the inn to meet with Gertie. Technically, the fact that she had five guests might very well be good for my business.

Late season guests were unusual. We did get a few folks coming through town in the fall for the color tour. Connecticut was practically a fireball with autumn colors almost all the way through to Halloween, if the winds weren't too bad. Unfortunately, that season had passed.

"Did you know that Oliver Bend is the town's treasurer?" Elsie asked me the question as if that piece of information meant something, when clearly I only ever knew the real reasons for the goings-on in this little town thanks to these two women. If they hadn't told me about Mr. Bend, then I wouldn't have known a thing about him. "Oliver just bought a cottage on the other side of the lake."

Wait. I *did* recognize the name Oliver, but just not his surname.

He was one of your grandmother's clients, though he hasn't been in to see you yet. Eczema on his elbows, I believe.

"Don't forget that his wife also bought a late model minivan last month," Wilma chimed in, always the follower of the two. It was now obvious what direction they were taking this conversation. "You tell us. Where do you think that they are getting that kind of money?"

"From their savings? Maybe an inheritance?" I couldn't help but smile as I grabbed my purse and the folder I'd worked on all night from underneath the counter. Pretty soon, these two ladies were going to announce that the mayor was an alien from another galaxy. It was a good thing they had no idea that the Marigolds didn't just dabble in herbal homeopathic remedies…we were the real deal. "Elsie and Wilma, Oliver and Alison are in their…what? Mid-sixties? I'm sure they've saved up some of their hard-earned money to enjoy their later years."

"Oliver said he took on the treasurer position to have something to do in his retirement," Elsie exclaimed, as if she were shocked that anyone would do such a thing.

"Then you should be happy for his selfless service to our community," I pointed out, wishing they didn't always think the worst of people. "You shouldn't be implying or creating tales about him stealing money from the town. Audits happen all the time as a way to discourage such behavior."

I don't know. They might have a point. Have you seen the

minivan that Alison Bend is driving? That thing is loaded to the gills.

Elsie and Wilma began to protest their innocence, given my subtle reprimand at their immediate judgement of a resident who was free to spend his own money as he saw fit. On the other hand, I was grateful they hadn't set their sights on me. I was also thankful that neither one of these ladies could hear Leo. He has a tendency to be a bit dramatic himself.

I am not dramatic.

"Would you like us to walk with you over to the inn?" Elsie asked, seemingly having forgotten that Wilma had spent whatever energy she had left buying the tea. I had no doubt that the elderly woman would feel better come morning with the help from the bewitching blend I'd created yesterday evening. "It's been a while since we've spoken with Gertie."

"Now Elsie, you just want to get a glimpse of those auditors and maybe be in a position to overhear what they have to say in regard to their reason for being here. I'm sure the audit is just standard procedure." I followed her and Wilma to the door before realizing that I'd forgotten my winter coat in the back room. "I appreciate the offer of company, but I think it's best that I take this meeting by myself. Besides, you really should get Wilma home and make her some of that tea. It wouldn't hurt for you to have a cup, as well. You never know."

Elsie regarded Wilma with a critical eye, but it wasn't like she could ignore her friend's red nose and puffy eyes.

"I need to grab my jacket, so you two go on ahead. Enjoy your tea."

Maybe they shouldn't leave quite yet.

Leo was usually snarky, so it was rare he used an apprehensive tone that had me stopping in my tracks. I spared a hesitant glance his way to find that he'd tilted his head, almost as if he were smelling the air for...danger?

I'm not sure, Leo answered me with a rather serious connotation.

His uncertainty had that intense burning in the palm of my hand that I had yet to figure out. I'd noticed the sensation the evening of my thirtieth birthday, but a lot had happened that night that I'd rather not get into right now.

You don't feel the electricity in the air?

By this time, Elsie and Wilma had vacated the shop. Their exit had let the cold breeze come in off the street. The black turtleneck I wore with my emerald green and black flowing skirt had done nothing to prevent goosebumps from breaking out all over my skin.

Was I simply cold or was I picking up the menacing force Leo seemed to catch with his slightly off-kilter nose?

My nose is fine, thank you.

It wasn't, but it was better to just go along with him.

"Leo, I'm not picking up anything unusual." I walked away from him before he could criticize the pace at which I was learning witchcraft. I was liable to disparage his ability as an instructor. That would only lead into another argument that I didn't have time for. "I'm late for my meeting. And seeing as this tea shop allows us to stay afloat, I'd best get moving."

It wasn't long before I'd shrugged into my new dress coat that Mindy had convinced me to buy the other day. I locked the front door of the tea shop after I'd stepped outside. I made sure my handmade sign was front and center, telling any potential customers that I would only be gone a half hour at most.

I stopped at the display window, ignoring the cold temperatures as I stared back at Leo. He'd moved from his spot and was now standing on all four paws. His ears were well-spanned apart, as if he were listening for something only he could hear.

I wished he'd chosen another day to do this to me. It wasn't fair that his odd behavior was leaving me worried that something might happen out of my control.

I deserved a little bit of peace and quiet, right?

I'd had a lot thrown at me in the short time I'd arrived in Paramour Bay, and I'd like to think I'd handled it with grace. My life had finally settled into a wonderful routine. I was making friends, the shop had a steady stream of business, and my mother was becoming used to the idea that I'd moved away from the city and was following along in the family traditions.

No, I wasn't going to let Leo's behavior worry me. He was more dramatic than those soap operas Elsie and Wilma made time to watch every afternoon while complaining that Paramour Bay wasn't nearly as exciting as those storylines on television.

I purposefully turned away from the display window and continued to walk down the sidewalk as I tucked the folder underneath my arm. My gloves were in my right pocket, so I quickly pulled them out and drew one of them over my still-tingling palm.

Ignorance was bliss, right?

Well, I could be the queen of ignorance.

Nothing was going to ruin my day or my upcoming first big sale.

Chapter Two

"GERTIE, IT'S NICE to finally meet you in person."

I meant every word of what I said, however it did take me a minute to get over my initial shock at her appearance. From the sound of the woman's voice on the phone, I was expecting someone in her mid-sixties.

Gertie Watson had to be well into her nineties, if not…well, many years older.

I made a mental note to ask Elsie and Wilma just how old the woman really was, considering she could have retired long before I was born. Truthfully, I was afraid she was going to lose her balance and fall to the ground due to her frail appearance.

Running any kind of business was rather strenuous, let alone a bed and breakfast where meals had to be prepped and served throughout the day, linens had to be laundered, and boarders and their accommodations needed attention from a well-trained staff daily. It made me tired just imagining all that went into keeping this establishment functioning effectively each and every day, let alone all those operations being supervised by woman who couldn't walk unassisted.

"Come in, dear." Gertie's cane shook as she slowly—and I mean slowly—turned away from the large seating area. Astonishingly, there wasn't a strand of grey hair out of place. I expected the interior to smell of mildew after seeing the woman's knotted hands, but there was a sweet flowery scent that was rather welcoming. "I was just overseeing the lunch preparations. I run a tight ship around here."

I was glad she'd prefaced the lunch preparations with the word *overseeing*. It was as if I could literally feel the arthritis settling into my joints at the thought of such physical labor three times a day, plus the additional chores that couldn't go ignored.

It was then it hit me as if I'd been jaywalking in New York City and a taxi cab had come out of nowhere and knocked me twenty feet into the air—my Nan had to be somehow responsible for Gertie's extraordinarily good health.

"I'll give you a tour of our little B&B in a bit, after we've concluded our business."

"I'd love that, Gertie," I replied sincerely, thinking of all the practice I'd get with Nan's spell book in the coming weeks. Were all the tea blends bewitched with a health and anti-aging enchantment or did Gertie get a special concoction straight from the spigot, so to speak? "What is that fragrance I smell? It's so…welcoming."

Okay. That wasn't the best adjective I could come up with, but the sweet scent did make me want to stay here forever. It was like walking through a field of wildflowers on a warm, sunny day with a faint refreshing breeze. My reaction truly was a contradiction.

You have to understand that the bed and breakfast resembled one of those New England haunted manors in those old budget horror movies that had a person tossing popcorn into the air when something went bump in the night. I expected there to be cobwebs in every corner, creaks shrilling out with every step, or some hidden passageway revealed with a flip of a lever.

And here I thought my overactive imagination had been

tamed after the past few months of anything but a mundane routine. Although, I *was* a witch…with a legacy running all the way back to the first Connecticut witch trials. Maybe I'd been expecting too much from my first big business meeting.

I continued to follow Gertie through the spacious area where the walls were lined with rich wood, antique furniture that could have come out of the early 1920s, and ancient Oriental silk area rugs that most likely cost more than all the items in the quaint stores along Main Street, including my tea shop.

The B&B was basically a historic two-story Cape Cod Gothic manor on the main thoroughfare coming into town across from the oddly located wax museum.

I know what you're thinking.

A wax museum in such a small town?

I found it oddly strange as well, but apparently my Nan helped out the institution through donations from time to time. I'd yet to hear who owned the place, but I'm sure they'll reach out to me come tax season or when they wanted to renew Nan's previous financial agreement with me.

Sorry.

I'm getting off topic.

Anyway, this historic home had been in Gertie's family for many generations. The inn had made several appearances in architectural and home décor magazines over the years, generating interest here and there from travelers all around the world.

Let's face it. Paramour Bay only had three hundred and fifty-four residents. Technically, the figure was three hundred and fifty-five if I counted myself. My point was that the town didn't get many strangers milling about River Bay, which was the main road in and out of town.

"Ms. Gertie, you have a beautiful place here," I said sincerely, wanting to keep the conversation flowing as we leisurely continued to walk toward the kitchen. It was hard for me not to put my hand on her arched back to ensure that she didn't fall, but she appeared to be a very prideful woman. "The traditional tapestry patterns etched on the furniture are absolutely stunning."

"Why, thank you, Raven. I was just telling Alison that it might be time to change things up a bit. My guests seem to get younger and younger as the years pass me by."

Alison? As in Oliver Bend's wife? Once again, I somehow managed to keep a straight face as the large kitchen came into view, revealing a woman who could only be Alison Bend. What were the odds? As far as I knew, there was no other Alison who resided in our small town.

What could she possibly be doing here at the inn?

I expected to hear Leo say something witty, but he was most likely scouring the streets for whatever had his whiskers tied in a knot today.

"Raven Marigold?" Alison stepped forward with a big smile on her face. No overt shadow of guilt was present that would even ever so slightly suggest she and her husband had done something to warrant the audit that was being conducted. She actually appeared to be a genuinely nice woman. "I'm Alison Bend. We haven't had a chance to meet you since your arrival, but your grandmother was a pillar of our community."

I take back my assessment.

Alison couldn't be that nice if she were willing to lie right to my face. Nan had been one of those women who others would call unique or distinctive. It hadn't been because she was a witch, but more so for her ability to be very direct. I was somewhat the same way, but I'd managed to curb that distinctive quality as it had a habit of upsetting the locals.

"It's nice to meet you, as well." I had taken off my coat and gloves in the front foyer, having plenty of time to hang my winter jacket on the antique coat rack. There had only been one hook left, which told me that the auditors were most likely in their rooms awaiting the noon meal. From my understanding, they'd only arrived in town today. They probably wouldn't be starting the audit until tomorrow morning. "Do you drink tea? You'll have to stop by the shop sometime."

"I usually only drink tea when I'm under the weather, but Gertie has just made us some Chai tea that is absolutely delicious," Alison praised a little too much, letting me know that she was trying to make an impression. She didn't need to do that, but her reasoning became clear when she continued the conversation. "I can't begin to tell you how generous your grandmother has been to the town's wax museum. She was always…"

A ringing sound set up residence in my ears and drowned out the rest of what Alison had to say about the odd institution located right at the city limit line. How could Leo not have told me that Alison Bend owned the wax museum? I'd mentioned numerous times how peculiar I found my Nan's interest in such a strange enterprise in such a small town.

Oh, that's right.

I forgot to mention that Leo has short-term memory loss from the dark magic my Nan had dabbled in to keep him on this earth beyond his natural time to help me transition into becoming a witch. Necromancy wasn't a sphere many white witches spent much time studying. That might serve to explain Leo's appearance.

Trust me, it wasn't easy going from being an average human

being to having the ability to cast spells.

"Anyway, I'd love a chance to sit down with you before the end of the year to talk about what continuing Rosemary's practice of making generous donations could do for the museum."

I smiled, unsure of how I was going to get out of this sour-pickled situation I'd found myself in. The shop had basically been closed for two weeks after Nan had passed away, so I was making up for lost time in the profit area. It also didn't help that I'd had to overcome a steep learning curve about tea leaves and how delicate a procedure it could be to get just the right blend.

Now would probably be a good time to mention that I'm a die-hard coffee drinker. I mean, I lived for the stuff when I resided in the city. Technically, I still do. The only one in town who knew of my dark roast secret was Liam. Sheriff Drake, to jog your memory. I still get warm all over at the memory of him actually bringing me a cup of coffee on my birthday. The man was certainly considerate, if nothing else.

"Raven," Gertie said somewhat in a bemused tone. She scooted her cane and slip-on shoes sluggishly until she could get a good look at me. "I just realized that your name starts with an R. I always thought it was coincidence with your grandmother and mother."

"The women in my family seem to have an odd sense of humor in that department," I admitted with an awkward laugh, still unsure what to make of Alison's presence. Why was she here? Had Oliver sent his wife to spy on the auditors? "I'm still discovering my lineage, but my great-grandmother's name was Rowena. Then came my Nan, Rosemary. And, of course, my mother's name is Regina."

"Will you continue the tradition?" Gertie's question seemed

rather out of place considering I hadn't had a date since moving to Paramour Bay. Her intense interest had me gripping the strap of my oversized bag I still had slung over my shoulder. "When you have children at some point, of course."

"I guess that would depend on my husband's level of forbearance." That answer should suffice, right? For some reason, I got the impression that Gertie was referencing the fact that neither my Nan or my mother had ever married. It was definitely time to change the subject. "Alison, will you be joining us to go over the B&B's annual order?"

"Oh, I was just picking up my granddaughter. Her car is in the shop. Leaky radiator."

As if they'd choreographed the next scene, a young girl with long blonde hair appeared from literally out of nowhere.

"Gertie, I'm going to go ahead and set out the fruit platters." She was young, maybe around twenty years of age. I'd never seen her before, but she did resemble Alison. "The finger sandwiches are also ready to go, but I won't put those trays out until you've taken a look at their presentation."

Gertie must really run a tight ship, and I could appreciate that given how many years she'd dedicated her life to her profession. She wanted it perfect. I understood her need to strive for excellence.

Let's face it. Nothing was worse than being the pariah of town.

Somehow, Alison was triggering my insecurities that I'd thought I'd been able to vanquish over the past two months.

"Thank you, Kimmie." Gertie motioned for me to take a seat at the large kitchen table that could have easily sat ten, though I'd seen a formal table twice this size out in the dining room. "Raven, please have a seat. I won't be but a second."

I wasn't so sure that was true, given that each step Gertie managed to take with her cane was at least thirty seconds each. I also didn't want to be alone with Alison, but it appeared that I didn't have much of a choice. It was easier for me to concentrate on pulling out the folder I'd brought with me that included a list of special tea blends she'd ordered in the past. Hopefully, Gertie would agree with the amount and price for these same items, and then I could be on my way.

"You're Raven Marigold," Kimmie said, not having followed Gertie to the other side of the kitchen and out of sight. The young girl's inquisitive gaze only added to my discomfort. "You're the one who moved here from New York City."

The way Kimmie spoke about the big city told me that she had big dreams. The hurt expression that crossed her grand-mother's face also told me that Kimmie's hopes for a life outside of Paramour Bay might be further down the road than she realized.

This was a battle that I wanted no part of.

"I am. Have you ever been to New—"

The bloodcurdling scream that echoed throughout the house was one I was very well acquainted with, though it had only ever developed in my head due to the sight of a body being discovered in the back of the tea shop.

Alison, Kimmie, and I all stared at one another in horror.

What could have caused such a reaction?

"What in the world?" Gertie exclaimed, shuffling back into view with a concerned expression written across her weathered features. "Did someone fall?"

I highly doubted a scream that loud came from someone slipping in a bathroom, but I didn't want to perpetuate the woman's fear that something horrible had just taken place inside her inn.

Ever since my thirtieth birthday, which happened to fall on Halloween, I'd somehow gotten a sixth sense about people, places, and things.

Right now?

The palm of my hand had heated to the point of discomfort.

We all rushed forward into the living room from the kitchen, leaving Gertie to slowly follow behind. No one was downstairs in the living room area, so it made sense that the scream had come from one of the bedrooms on the second floor. We had just reached the landing at the bottom of the stairwell when a pretty woman wearing an off-white pantsuit came barreling down the steps, her face as pale as the fabric of her jacket.

"H-he's dead." The woman put a hand out on the railing to steady herself. It was evident that she'd had a shock to her system. I tried very hard to convince myself that whoever she was talking about had died of natural causes, but the look of disbelief and dismay that crossed her features told a different story. "Someone murdered Ben Stanway."

This couldn't be happening.

Not again.

I was beginning to feel like the Schleprock from "The Flintstones".

That trend I spoke about earlier this morning had decided to rear its ugly head again. Even though this time I wasn't the one who had found the body, there went my hope for any semblance of peace in Paramour Bay.

Chapter Three

"IF YOU WANTED a cup of coffee that bad, all you had to do was walk over to the station," Liam muttered in an attempt to soothe my anxiety.

Unfortunately, it didn't help.

Nothing was going to ease my apprehension that another murder had taken place in the span of two months, both in close proximity to myself. Granted, one didn't have anything to do with the other, but that didn't make any of this okay.

People were bound to believe that I was a pariah in Paramour Bay, even if I hadn't done anything wrong. It wouldn't surprise me if I became an outcast amongst the townspeople. Did such things still happen in the twenty-first century? Was I going to be run out of town on a rail?

"I don't think my stomach could handle anything that acidic at the moment." I'd been nauseous ever since I'd heard that bloodcurdling scream echo throughout this old house. I could still hear the remaining tentacles of the piercing shriek creeping down my spine. "I can't believe this is happening. Is there any news?"

Liam ran a hand over his face as he joined me in the corner of the large living room. His smile wasn't as comforting as I'd hoped it would be. He was probably trying to make this moment easier for me, but it wasn't going to work. I'd found myself caught up in another murder investigation, and there wasn't a thing I could do to preempt it.

"As you've probably heard, Ben Stanway was the victim. He was one of the auditors sent here from the state auditor's office. He was in charge of the assessment, as well as the team he'd brought with him."

I bit my tongue to keep from asking Liam if he thought Alison Bend had anything to do with Mr. Stanway's murder, but I couldn't bring myself to verbalize such an accusation. She was the obvious choice, though. Let's face it. Oliver Bend was the treasurer of Paramour Bay, and the town was about to get audited after years under Oliver's tenure. His wife had obviously been present at the time the crime was committed.

I don't think it will take a genius to figure this one out.

With that said, I really needed to stay as far away from this investigation as possible. At least, for my own selfish reasons, of course. The town was still leery of anyone new coming to town, regardless that I was the granddaughter of the infamous Rosemary Marigold.

Besides, adding to the body count would surely cut down on the casual walkthrough traffic of my tea shop.

Being banished wasn't such a farfetched notion, was it?

"I heard one of the officers say that the man was stabbed to death." It was rather hard to swallow around the constriction that had formed in my throat. I hadn't been going to voice my opinion, but that was something I struggled with after having lived in New York City. "Alison was in the kitchen with us. You don't think she…"

I let my voice trail off, not wanting to outright accuse the woman of murder. I didn't have to point out that she had access to a knife. That much was obvious. Wait. I *had* just essentially accused her of murdering Ben Stanway out loud.

Oh, this wasn't going to end well for me.

I should really excuse myself and head back to the tea shop, but I'd yet to give my statement to the detective who was currently speaking with some of the auditors across the room.

As for Alison, she was sitting on one of those sofas that I'd admired upon my arrival. She was clutching her granddaughter's hands, though Kimmie wasn't paying any attention to the woman. The young lady was too busy staring up the staircase at the various law enforcement officers and technicians coming and going like itsy-bitsy ants scouring the landscape for any sign of a clue.

"I'm sure that the townsfolk will spread rumors about Alison being here at the time of the murder, just as I'm sure they will note your presence. But there's no evidence to prove that she—or you, for that matter—had anything to do with Ben Stanway's death. Her clothes don't have a drop of blood on them."

And that, right there, was why I wasn't a police officer. I hadn't even thought to look over Alison Bend's apparel for blood splatter. Another wave of nausea rolled through my stomach. I didn't want to think about the body upstairs or the surrounding scene. What a horrible way to die…having holes punched into you until you leaked like a sieve.

"The body was still warm when I arrived, so whoever did stab the victim had done so sometime this morning and not earlier during the night." Liam nodded toward the detective who'd been called in when Heidi and I had discovered a body in the storage room of the tea shop. Detective Swanson was apparently still on rotation to take on any new cases in Paramour Bay. I had noticed right away that his gaze had landed on me, most likely making the easy connection I was once again involved in a murder investigation. I never did have the best of luck. "I'm sure Jack will solve this one quickly."

Jack must be Detective Swanson, though I'd never heard his first name mentioned before. Liam called the detective in on cases that the local sheriff's department couldn't handle due to their limited resources. Let's face it—Paramour Bay didn't have the ability to pay for new parking meters, let alone foot the bill for forensics or the manpower required to oversee a murder investigation.

My presence here had to have the good detective wondering if I was somehow involved or if I had just fallen into a pit of bad luck.

Honestly, it could be both at this stage.

"The suspect pool isn't very deep." I don't know why I said something so insensitive, but the detective's steady gaze was making me quite uncomfortable. I crossed my legs and hooked my hands around my knee in order to give me something to do. "I mean, maybe one of Mr. Stanway's colleagues is the guilty party."

"Jack is taking everyone's statements now." Liam's dark gaze swung my way. I did my best not to react in a guilty manner, even though I had nothing to do with this murder. I chalked up my reaction to that of a teenage driver traveling just below the speed limit when passing a police car. It was instinctive to tap my brakes, even though I hadn't been doing anything wrong. "You'll have to give a statement of your own, Raven."

"I think I'm the last one left who hasn't done so already."

Liam looked as if he wanted to say something, but he just as quickly snapped his teeth together. I didn't have to be a witch to know what was on his mind.

"Go ahead," I encouraged, wishing he'd just get it over with.

There went my hope for a date. I could see his brown eyes darkening with humor, so I knew I was on the right track. "Just say it. I'm bad luck."

Liam studied me a little too intently, and my stomach fluttered in response.

Okay.

Maybe I was wrong.

Was Liam finally going to ask me out on a date in spite of the fact that I tended to find myself smackdab in the middle of everything that had gone wrong around here?

"Ms. Marigold." Detective Swanson made an appearance sooner than I'd expected. I tried not to frown at the timing. He might take it the wrong way. "I'm sorry that we're meeting again under such similar circumstances."

And there it was.

The tiny little dig that I'd managed to get caught up in one of his cases again.

"I was only here to meet with Gertie about her annual tea order." I hadn't wanted to come across so defensively, but I'd utterly failed. It was becoming a very bad habit that I was going to need to break sooner rather than later. I certainly didn't want to end up behind bars for a crime I didn't commit. "We were all in the kitchen when we heard Ms. Duggan scream before she came running down the stairs."

Rachel Duggan was the woman in the off-white pantsuit who'd scrambled down the stairs after discovering Ben Stanway on the floor with a knife in the middle of his chest. I couldn't help but think back to that moment, wondering if there had been any blood on her clothes. I couldn't recall seeing any, but then again, I hadn't been looking at the woman all that closely.

Liam's previous comment had made sure that from this

point forward I would forever look for blood on a person if I were ever in a situation like this again. Not that I ever intended to be near another homicide right after it happened.

No. I was done with dead bodies and homicide investigations.

Rachel Duggan caught my attention when she walked over to Gertie. She was still wearing the business suit, but no stains appeared to be on the fabric. Now that my thoughts had taken me there, who wore white in the middle of winter, anyway? Technically, it was the beginning of winter. Labor Day had, in fact, passed. Still, my mother's warning about not wearing white after the first week of September had been burned into my brain.

"Who was included in that *we?*" Detective Swanson asked, bringing my attention back around to the interrogation. At least, that's what this felt like. The tip of his pen was touching the pad of paper he always seemed to carry inside his suit jacket. His question did have me thinking back to when Ms. Duggan had screamed in horror. *Had* Ben been murdered while I'd been in the kitchen? I couldn't suppress the shudder that went through my shoulders. "And what time did you arrive?"

I spent the next five minutes giving my account of the last couple of hours, which was how long I'd been sitting here waiting for the state police to arrive. Eileen, who was Paramour Bay's police dispatcher, had retrieved Liam from the diner immediately. He had every guest downstairs, a call put into Detective Swanson, and the upstairs cut off from the guests in attendance in a matter of minutes. He was very efficient that way.

And no, there wasn't any blood on their clothes. I'd already checked over the rest of the guests, leaving it a true mystery of who had actually stabbed Ben Stanway.

The four other auditors who had booked rooms at the inn beside Mr. Stanway were Rachel Duggan, Valerie Jacoba, Neal Edlyn, and David Laken. Three of them were currently huddled in the corner, most likely trying to figure out who could be to blame for their supervisor's murder, as well as what implications remained. Rachel was just now rejoining them after having spoken to Gertie.

All of them looked Alison's way.

Again, I couldn't help but agree with the obvious suspect.

"How is your friend doing in New York City?"

Detective Swanson took me by surprise with his question, although Liam didn't seem to blink an eye. It took me a moment to word my answer, because I hadn't been aware of the man's interest in my best friend.

"Um, she's doing okay. Heidi mentioned visiting me this coming weekend." I really wanted to leave for the tea shop, but I didn't want it to look as if I were trying to run away from this conversation. If that meant throwing Heidi under the proverbial bus, then so be it. My best friend was a New Yorker through and through. She could handle herself in any situation, and she would totally agree about me taking the lifeboat offered. "I'm sure you'll see her around town. She's going to help me with my inventory count. Speaking of which, I really do need to get back to the shop. I've been closed most of the afternoon, and that isn't exactly good for business. I'll tell Heidi you asked after her, though."

"I'll walk Raven out," Liam offered, following my lead. He rested a hand on my lower back when I finally stood from the couch. I don't think he's ever touched me, with the exception of our fingers brushing against each other the day he'd brought me coffee. "I'll also make sure that the crowd outside goes on their merry way."

"Don't forget to reach out to Otis," Detective Swanson reminded him, bringing up the former sheriff. "He'll want to be briefed on what happened."

I held back my sigh of relief that I was finally going to be able to leave the inn. My palm had literally begun physically hurting instead of just containing that warm sensation I'd become accustomed to, and it was beginning to scare me.

I really needed to talk to Leo about it, as well as numerous other things. He was a wealth of information, though his short-term memory loss was rather burdensome halfway through his sentences.

"Here," Liam said, reaching out for my winter jacket that was still hanging up on the antique coat rack. "Let me help you with this."

I set down my oversized bag so that I could offer him my arm, shifting slightly to slip my hand through the sleeve. It didn't take me long to fasten one of the middle buttons and adjust my scarf. I wasn't surprised to find that everyone's gaze was on me by the time I'd finished. I'm sure they all wished they could leave this crime scene, too.

Liam lifted my purse so that I didn't have to bend back down, his gesture telling me that his mother had raised a gentleman. I gave him a small smile at future possibilities, but that quickly faded when Gertie came shuffling into view with her cane.

"Raven, dear, I don't know what to say," Gertie exclaimed with a slow shake of her head. Her blue eyes filled with tears. It was more than apparent she was beside herself over the tragedy that had taken place right here in her B&B. "This is horrible, just horrible."

"Gertie, if you need anything, anything at all, please let me know." I wasn't sure what I could do, but I did feel bad for the elderly woman. I understood exactly what it was like to have a murder occur in my place of business. "Don't worry about the tea order. We can get together when everything dies down."

I hadn't realized what I'd said until Liam gently nudged me in the arm.

Shoot.

My mouth sometimes worked ahead of my brain.

Now wasn't the time to talk business.

"You can go ahead and fill the order with whatever you believe my guests will prefer, Raven. I trusted your grandmother, and I trust you," Gertie said somewhat distractedly, all of her attention on the front door where Oliver Bend made an entrance. "Oh, dear."

"Alison? Alison, darling, are you alright?"

Oliver was rather on the short side, maybe only an inch taller than my five-foot, six-inch frame. His wire-rimmed glasses had slid down the bridge of his nose, allowing for everyone to see the concern shining brightly in his bulging blue eyes. He made a direct beeline for his wife and granddaughter, but his attention had veered to Detective Swanson.

It was hard not to notice that his concern was rather short-lived.

"What happened here? I shouldn't have had to hear from my wife that there's been a murder where our granddaughter works." Oliver huffed in annoyance as he took one of Alison's hands away from Kimmie. "Alison, are you alright?"

"I'm fine, I'm fine," Alison assured her husband, appearing a bit uncomfortable by all the attention. She stood before helping Kimmie to her feet. "Oliver, I think it's best we let the police handle this however they see fit. Besides, Kimmie is too young to be around all…this."

I was slightly confused with Oliver's exclamation.

What authority did Oliver believe he had over the town's police department that he should be notified about certain investigations?

No. I was going to forget the direction my thoughts had taken me. I didn't want to know anything about Oliver Bend, his job, or why the state wanted an audit.

"I think it's time for me to go." My curiosity was piqued, and that wasn't always a good thing. I had secrets of my own to worry about, and me being involved in another murder would only draw more scrutiny my way. "I really should be getting back to the shop."

Liam once again rested a hand on my lower back as he escorted me through the front door, seemingly oblivious to Oliver's proclamation. I did have to wonder where the crowd of gatherers had come from, considering it was in the middle of a workday and most folks should be back at work from their lunchbreaks. I think the only ones who weren't in attendance were Elsie and Wilma. I could only imagine their reaction upon hearing the gory details.

"Two homicides in the span of a month," Liam muttered in disbelief, walking me down the steps of the beautiful B&B. The cold wind almost took my breath away, but it was also rather refreshing. Anything was better than being cooped up in that place with too many people crowded in the living room. "This town has gone fifty-three years without one until this year. If I believed in astrology, I'd think Mercury was in retrograde."

It was a good thing he *didn't* believe in that kind of stuff. I'd have a lot of explaining to do, otherwise. It wasn't much of a leap from having a belief in astrology to modern day witchcraft.

I wish Liam hadn't reminded me of that cold case from so long ago. He'd mentioned a couple months previously that my Nan had actually been a person of interest in that investigation, though nothing had ever come to fruition. I'd been so busy with learning my new trade that I'd left it to the powers that be.

To be truthful, I was afraid I would find answers I didn't want to know.

"Raven," a female voice called out. I immediately recognized it as Mindy Walsh. "Raven, over here!"

"You know these people better than me, Liam." I held up a hand to Mindy that I would join her shortly. "Are they going to ostracize me for being in the wrong place at the wrong time?"

"I'm sorry, Raven. I didn't mean to upset you or make you think that you're not welcome here." Liam must have thought his talk about two murders in the span of five weeks was what had me concerned. It did make me wonder at the odd string of events, but Mr. Stanway's death had nothing to do with witchcraft or my tea shop. I was more concerned about the townsfolk's opinion me. "You were just unlucky enough to be here when someone discovered the body. No one is going to ostracize you."

Don't bet on it. Do you see the way Cora Barnes is looking at you?

Leave it to Leo to show up now. I hadn't seen him in the crowd of people, but I had no doubt that he was somewhere nearby.

Unfortunately, Leo was right.

Cora Barnes hadn't liked me since my arrival, but that had more to do with her animosity toward my mother. That was another long story that I'd have to get into later, but just so you're aware, Cora and Desmond Barnes owned the malt shop that was located in between my tea shop and Mindy's boutique.

I'm always right. I also told you that you shouldn't have left the store this morning, didn't I? Now look at what you've gotten yourself caught up in.

I wasn't going to give Leo the satisfaction of telling him that he was right twice in one day.

"I'd walk you back to the shop, but I told Jack that I'd help him wrap up this crime scene. Gertie still has guests that need to gain access to their rooms." Liam scanned the crowd, giving away his intention to keep his word about clearing out the residents who had gathered around the sidewalk of the inn. "Those auditors still have a job to do, and it's not like they have anywhere else to stay while they're in town."

"You mean, the audit will still take place after all this?"

Stop asking questions. The last thing we need is for the good sheriff to think you're involved with another murder.

"Yes." Liam surveyed the crowd in front of him, causing me to do the same. He was right. Pretty much everyone in town was right here at the inn. "It was ordered by the state. Trust me, the audit will continue. Isn't that your cat over there?"

Sure enough, Leo was on the outer band of the residents gathered round so that they didn't miss a thing. Maybe if I brushed him a bit, he'd look a little better.

You're not getting anywhere near me with a brush. Besides, I think I'm rocking this body.

"Leo was probably lonely." I offered up the excuse, because it was the only one that sprang to mind. Heidi was better at retorts than I was, and I'm sure she'd have one or two in response to Detective Swanson's interest. Her last relationship hadn't ended well. Men were lower than dirt right now in Heidi's opinion. "I should be getting back to the shop. Thank you, Liam, for everything."

I truly meant the appreciation I expressed, because I wasn't sure how well I would have handled another murder without Liam's reassurance that everything was going to be okay. Not being much of a natural at this witch thing had my confidence a little down, and I'm not so sure I would have answered Detective Swanson's questions with such ease.

"Raven?" Liam had reached out for my arm when I went to join Mindy in the crowd. Don't think for a minute I was going to stay until the coroner removed the body. All I was going to do was invite Mindy to the house tonight. It would be good for me get my mind off of today's events. "Would you like to have dinner with me sometime?"

Did the good ol' sheriff just ask you out on a date?

Had he?

I'd waited close to two months for just this moment, though it had never occurred to me that it would take place at another crime scene. I probably looked like a fool standing in front of him with my mouth hanging open.

Let's just say that you don't look your best.

"Yes," I replied quickly, wondering if there was a spell to get rid of sarcasm. "Yes, I'd love to have dinner with you sometime."

No, you wouldn't. What are you thinking? Did we not just go through one investigation where you had trouble hiding your lineage? You always seem to forget that you have obligations that you can't just...

"You mentioned Heidi was coming to visit this weekend, so maybe we can get together after she heads back to the city?" Liam asked, not knowing that his words were drowning out the irritating lecture I was receiving. "And I'll even make sure there's coffee available."

"I already said yes, but that last part was definitely the clincher."

I returned his infectious smile, but it slowly faded as he looked over his shoulder toward the front door of the inn. It was still wide open and being guarded by a uniformed officer, who never once took his gaze off the gathered crowd.

We said our goodbyes, both of us walking toward the locals still gathered on the sidewalk. He began telling them that there was nothing for them to see, and that he would give a statement to the local newspaper later today about all that had taken place this morning.

Liam then reassured the residents that they were still safe in Paramour Bay, and that this was nothing like the previous investigation that had resulted in one of their own being incarcerated in a state-run mental institution.

...and if that's all it takes, I'll teach you a spell that turns tea into coffee. I can't believe you said yes. When will you learn that...

Leo was like a broken record, but I was getting better and better at tuning out his drawn-out reprimands. I began walking over toward Mindy, who was listening intently to what Liam had to say. My knee-high boots felt like they were stepping on puffy clouds. There wasn't a thing Leo could say or do that could take away my excitement over what had just taken place.

...something just came to me. Oh, this is bad. Real bad.

I repeated to myself that nothing Leo could say or do could ruin my day.

I should have known that wasn't the case.

Ben Stanway was one of your grandmother's clients.

Chapter Four

I PULLED UP to my house on the edge of town, right inside the town's limit. The roads out here weren't too bad for this time of year, but I'd heard chatter on the radio about a possible snowstorm arriving later in the week. There was still ample time to gather some supplies that I was lacking in the grocery department, but every day that the shop wasn't open presented a lost opportunity to get the books out of the red and back into the black. There never seemed to be enough hours in the day to get everything done.

At this point, I was too exhausted to do anything other than have a glass of wine.

"I know you can hear me, Leo."

I scanned the property that was a good half-mile away from civilization, taking in the eerie sight that was my home. It would put off most people. To be fair, the exterior looked even more bleak in the winter than the summer.

Don't get me wrong. It wasn't Norman Bates' house on the hill, but it did have that Halloween creepy house-in-the-woods vibe.

Nan had probably gotten a kick out of the fact that the place resembled a witch's cottage in some fairytale, when no one truly had any idea that she could really cast unnerving spells that would have any sensible person running in the opposite direction.

You see, a wrought iron fence surrounded the small area out front that had two stark trees on either side. The naked branches had lost their leaves earlier this fall, but the bark seemed to darken the more we entered the colder months.

It was almost as if the gnarled trees were competing with the fence as to what item could cause the property to look more ominous than the gates of hell. The pillars of the wrought iron won hands down. Those sharp spikes on the top of each post were downright menacing, if you really studied them.

The dreary scene before me technically summed up my mood, because it took all of my might not to indulge myself with the scream of frustration that had been brewing since I'd left the inn earlier today.

"Leo, you can't hide from me forever." I didn't bother to hide my frustration. "You're the scarecrow, not the lion. Have a bit of courage."

I'm not so sure the familiar had been prepared for the tongue lashing I'd given him once we'd gotten back to the tea shop. Mindy ended up not getting her invitation. I was too angry that Leo had kept such important information from me.

It's not my fault, you know. You can blame Rosemary and her lack of mastering the spell she used on me. She's the one who caused my short-term memory loss.

Leo suddenly appeared outside the front gate. I slammed the door shut to my old Chevy with all my might to prevent myself from launching at him and pulling out one bent whisker at a time.

"You can't use short-term memory loss as an excuse every time you decide to withhold information from me, Leo. Ben Stanway wasn't even listed in Nan's client book, and—"

"You two are fighting."

I stomped my foot to keep myself from screaming in surprise at the deep voice that always came out of nowhere.

Every. Single. Time.

"Ted, you need to stop sneaking up on me. I'm not to be trifled with tonight."

Now was probably a good time for me to explain who Ted was and how I came to inherit him, along with Nan's cottage at the edge of town.

Let me emphasize—Ted literally came with the house.

It would also give my heart a chance to slow down so I didn't spring a leak. I certainly didn't want to have a heart attack at the age of thirty before I'd had a chance to find out who I really was considering all the recent developments.

With my awful luck, I'd barely survive and be stuck in a wheelchair with all the medical bills instead.

Anyway, you know those great big giants you read about in fairy tales?

Well, that pretty much described Ted to a tee, except he was rather insightful at times. I'm still not certain he was completely human, but I wasn't ready to know what he was until I had more of a handle on this witchcraft stuff and why Nan wanted me here.

What we don't know can't hurt us, right?

At least, that's the motto I've come up with in regard to Ted.

He was at least six feet, six inches tall...if not more when the moon was full. His yellowish blond hair was always the same shade and length, regardless of the amount of time since his last visit to town. I'll admit to being curious about whether or not his hair ever grew, but not enough to actually ask or look into the matter.

Ted had a penchant for suits cut in the style of the late 1800s, and he even had a paisley handkerchief stuffed in the outer pocket of his jacket. It gave him an air of being an old-fashioned gentleman, which he truly was in almost every aspect.

His manners were impeccable.

Then there was the fact that he conveyed his thoughts in rather concise sentences. That trait had been annoying at first, but I now found it rather endearing.

A gentleman? Endearing? Are you kidding me? Do you really want to know what he is?

"Oh, now you can remember stuff? I'm beginning to think these memory lapses are more of some contrived excuse that you use when you're spinning your own ulterior motives," I muttered, purposefully not addressing Leo's question and reaming him about earlier. "You knew Ben Stanway was one of Nan's clients, and you purposefully didn't tell me that fact before I walked over to the inn. Why would you hide that information?"

"I didn't mean to startle you," Ted interrupted, somehow opening the gate without having the hinges squeak as they always did.

He's lying. He did mean it. He enjoys sneaking up on you.

"I know you didn't, Ted. Somehow, you have a knack for doing it anyway," I replied tiredly, actually considering going to bed early. Tomorrow was a new day, right? "You'll have to teach me that trick someday."

It's not something you can learn. You see, Ted is a—

"Leo is certainly animated this evening."

I might have forgotten to mention that Ted couldn't hear Leo's side of the conversation. Only witches in our lineage have that dubious privilege. I guess that marked off witch as being one of the things Ted could be. Anyway, all that Ted heard was a chorus of meows, one right after another as Leo tried to dig his way out of this hole.

Privilege? Really? And who wanted to eradicate sarcasm?

"Ignore him, Ted. He's managed to ruin my entire day." I pushed off my car and began to walk forward, no longer wanting to remain out here in the cold. The temperature had dropped significantly all day. My fingers and toes were almost numb, but that was mostly because the heater in my car was on the fritz. It had a mind of its own, and only worked when it wanted to. "I have a mind to lock Leo outside tonight."

You wouldn't be that cruel.

"Try me," I warned with a squint, not caring that both of us knew that I'd never do such a thing. It was still a point I was trying to make. "Ted, did you know that Ben Stanway was one of Nan's clients?"

"Yes."

Once again, I forced the scream of frustration down my throat. There was no going to bed early. I really needed a glass of wine to chase away my irritation.

"And no one thought to tell me this vital bit of information?"

"Why does it matter?"

See? I'm not the only one who doesn't think it's that big of a deal.

Leo swished his bent tail as gracefully as he could in what I assume was supposed to be a regal fashion. It didn't quite have the look he was hoping for as he barged his way into the house.

"It matters because Ben Stanway came to town to do an audit on Paramour Bay today, and he ended up being stabbed to death in his room at the inn." I still couldn't believe that I'd been there when Mr. Stanway's body was discovered. I couldn't prevent the shudder that went through my shoulders, but that could have been because I'd just removed my winter jacket. "Ben Stanway is dead, Ted."

Did you really just rhyme that?

"His protection spell must have worn off," Ted said matter-of-factly, as if he hadn't just dropped another bombshell.

That was two sucker punches in one day.

I wasn't sure I could take any more.

"Protection spell?" I had been in the process of pulling down the zipper on one of my knee-high boots when I caught Leo halting the swagger of his hips in the middle of the room. His tail gradually lowered as he looked over his right shoulder to where Ted was still standing near the door. "You truly don't remember what Nan did for him, do you, Leo?

I recall Ben Stanway coming into the store at different times.

Leo somehow managed to move only his back paws until he was facing me. He then sat back on his hunches with a plop. His eyes somehow bulged even more than when in their natural state.

I don't remember their conversation exactly.

It was then I recognized the panic that had settled into Leo's large green eyes. My guilt began to build. His current anxiety level was similar to what I'd experienced when Rachel Duggan had come barreling down the stairs of the B&B.

"Leo, I'm sorry. I was very harsh on you today. I'm feeling a bit lost with everything that has happened this morning, and it wasn't fair of me to take my bad mood out on you." I dropped my boot before working on the other. Within seconds, my cozy slippers were doing their best to warm up my toes. It wasn't an easy feat considering my entire body had gone cold with dread upon hearing this recent discovery. "Ted, could you shed some light on why Ben Stanway thought he needed a protection spell?"

"I don't think so."

It was rare that Leo got worked up to the point that he resembled a feral cat. The sight of his broken and chipped claws baring themselves told me just how upset he truly was after today's events.

His whiskers were also twitching, and that was always a telltale sign that he was ready to act without thinking.

"Leo," I warned before putting myself in between him and Ted. "We'll figure this out given enough time."

Figure this out? A second client of your grandmother is dead. Dead. Do you know what the odds of that are? I know the number, but I'm too upset right now to remember it. And you just agreed to go out with the sheriff, who has no idea that you're a real witch. This is...

I allowed Leo to go on and on, venting out his frustration on a situation that I wasn't even certain we were a part of. Neither was he, but he didn't seem to remember that at the moment.

Leo was right, in a way.

Okay—a major way, though I still wasn't going to give him full credit.

It didn't look good that Ben Stanway had been Nan's client, but the man's name had never been recorded in the book that she'd used for her orders. Liam would never make the connection, leaving us in the free and clear.

Right?

"Ted, please don't stand by the door. It makes me nervous. Come have a seat at the counter."

I would have offered Ted something to eat, but he always

turned me down. As a matter of fact, I've never observed him eating food or allowing any drink past his thin lips and a couple of broken teeth.

Would you be able to eat with those choppers?

"Ted, would you please tell me what you remember about Ben Stanway?" I walked around Leo, who was still shooting an evil glare at Ted. Maybe with a little bit of guidance, I could get Ted to recall something of use. "Anything would help."

By habit, one that mostly came from previously finding a dead body in the back of my tea shop, I glanced over the beautiful interior of the cottage to make sure nothing was out of place.

I know what you're thinking—how could a house that appeared so hideous on the outside look so good on the inside?

Well, Nan loved the finer things in life. She just hadn't advertised that fact. Even though the tea shop brought in a nice, tidy profit...that was nothing compared to what she'd made selling her special tea blends that had a touch of her magic. I'm almost ashamed to admit that I thought she was dealing drugs after finding a list of her more intimate clients.

Anyway, Nan adored designer clothes, expensive furniture, and beautiful décor. She had gone all out with the most appealing modern furniture mixed with some antique pieces here and there as accents. The splashes of color made the place come alive, though my personal favorite was the coffee table.

The carved wood was unlike anything I'd ever seen. The piece had obviously been handmade with intricate carvings that just begged to be traced. Oh, and the coffee table also had special hiding places that made me realize there was much more to explore here than first met the eye.

Unfortunately, I wouldn't be doing any treasure hunting

tonight.

I made my way to the refrigerator and took out the cracker and cheese platter I'd made last night. I ended up not eating any of it, because I'd been too excited putting together a list for Gertie.

I never did place her order this afternoon.

I wasn't sure the elderly woman had actually meant it when she'd said she trusted my judgement to complete her order myself.

What if Gertie had just been in shock after finding out a murder had taken place in one of her bedrooms? What if she hadn't realized what she was authorizing me to do? It was best I wait and meet with her again after Liam or the state police solved the case and things settled down.

Unfortunately, I might not have a choice but to involve myself into this investigation. Ted seemed to know more than he was telling, but that wasn't unusual. I just had to ask the right questions.

"Ted? Can you remember anything that would help solve his murder?"

"Mr. Stanway was in fear for his life, of that I'm sure." Ted behaved as if he hadn't just dropped another bomb. Leo and I stared at him as he finally made it across the open space of the main floor. He took a seat on the stool rather stiffly, which was his usual manner of movement. "That is all I know."

He knows more. We could always torture it out of him.

I turned my back on both of them to get my thoughts in order. I took my time choosing the right bottle of wine in the rack above the stove. I didn't drink very often, usually only when I was with Heidi on the weekends, but once in a while I needed a little something to help me relax.

There had also been a study done that stated one glass of red wine in the evening was actually beneficial to one's health. Who was I to deny my body the benefits of the antioxidants and vitamins?

"Ted, how did Ben Stanway even know about Nan's side business?"

Nan had created a name for herself in the alternative medicine arena, but there were a handful of residents who believed she had a special *gift*. Not in true witchcraft, per se. No one knew that little particular secret of the Marigold family. As Leo had once told me—dabbling in witchcraft is totally different than being an actual witch.

It's good to know you listen to me once in a blue moon.

As usual, I ignored Leo and continued to look for the corkscrew that I'd used a couple of days ago. It wasn't in the dishwasher and it wasn't in the side drawer where I usually stashed it.

I might have knocked it off the counter and under the fridge.

Sure enough, the metal corkscrew was lying on the floor underneath the lip of the refrigerator.

Leo stretched out on the black granite, giving me a discerning look.

What can I say? It was shiny, and it was taunting me.

"I don't know." Ted's answer was becoming rather repetitive, so I asked him to tell me about the time Nan brought up the name in his presence. "Oh, she was very happy. Mr. Stanway paid double the usual rate."

Now we were getting somewhere.

"What else did Nan tell you?"

"Mr. Stanway was in town to meet Mr. Bend."

"When was this?" I opened the cupboard and pulled down

one of the wine glasses I had on the shelf in a small hex-shaped rack. "Nan moved on in October, so maybe over the summer?"

"It was warm outside." Ted shifted his ramrod straight shoulders as he sat back on the stool. He was always pale, but the overhead lighting didn't help his cause. "It was when Ms. Rosemary used that *black magic*."

What?

Ted's whisper of those two vile words had Leo's tail twitching. It wasn't long before he was on all fours, pacing back and forth on the counter.

No wonder I didn't remember good ol' Ben. Do you know how long it took me to recover from that horrid spell? Weeks, I tell you. Weeks.

I had been about to take a sip of my wine when something occurred to me. I'm not sure why I never asked about it before, but it wasn't something I was willing to let slide any longer than necessary.

"Leo, did—"

Don't ask something you're not ready to know.

I did pause, but only long enough to shrug off Leo's warning. It wasn't like I hadn't already accepted my lot in pursuing this life.

I was a witch.

I was learning new things every day and doing the best I could to adjust to this secretive journey I'd begun a little less than two months ago.

"Leo, did Nan know she was going to die?"

Chapter Five

"MOM, DO YOU know when you're going to die? I mean, do you know the actual date?"

I hadn't meant to ask the question so bluntly, but I couldn't help myself. Her potential response had been on my mind all night, causing me to toss and turn until I finally directed my attention to the spell book in search of a sleeping incantation or maybe a restoration spell of some sort.

Needless to say, that hadn't quite worked out the way I'd hoped.

I was wearing a little bit more foundation today than usual to hide the bags under my eyes.

"Not yet," Regina said rather cautiously over the phone connection. She probably knew where I was headed with this conversation. "Raven, what is that cat spouting on about now?"

Now I have a headache. Why did you have to call her?

I flipped the sign to the tea shop over so that it read *Open*, unable to keep myself from looking across the street at the police station where Liam might be lurking about. Eileen was unlocking the door, all bundled up in a knit hat, scarf, and gloves. There was no sign of Liam.

Maybe he left town, though I doubt I'd be that lucky.

"Nan knew well enough to cast a spell that would keep Leo here to help me adjust." I wasn't sure I would call what Leo provided as *help*, but he was better than nothing at all. "That means Nan saw her own death, doesn't it?"

Why are you asking your mother these questions? She ran off and left Rosemary all on her own, deprived of her daughter and grandchild. Regina shouldn't even be a part of this conversation. She deserted your grandmother.

"Mom's coming around, isn't she?" I whispered back, covering the bottom of the cell phone with my palm. I was trying to make a point, but Leo didn't seem to want to hear it or maybe he didn't care enough to listen. You see, my mother left Paramour Bay when she was in her early twenties. She never looked back, either. She'd wanted nothing to do with this witchcraft business and sought to make a normal life for herself...and me. As you can see, that decision hadn't turned out very well for her. "Patience, Leo."

"If you're in tune with the earth and its energy, then yes...you can be made aware of when your time on this earth is concluding, but only close to your natural end," Regina answered with enough tension in her voice that told me she didn't want to talk about it. A spike of fear pierced my heart. Was her death soon? I was afraid to ask. "How far along are you in learning the craft?"

Not far.

"It's going pretty good."

No, it's not.

"I made a tea blend to help Wilma with her immune system, casting a spell to rid her of the cold she's been fighting off."

You also caught your blouse on fire with a candle.

I spun around so fast that all four of Leo's paws came off the floor in surprise. He gathered his composure and huffed before strolling toward the storage room to sharpen his claws on the wooden shelving. It was a good thing he left me to my private conversation or else I wouldn't have been held responsible for my actions. I usually had to fight the urge to put another crook in his mangy old tail.

"Heidi is coming to visit me on Friday," I said, hoping to convince my mother to do the same. She was a wealth of information when it came to witchcraft, but it was like pulling teeth with her. I didn't want to have to do it all on my own, but my mother still wanted nothing to do with anything supernatural. That included this conversation. "Why don't you drive up with her? We can make it a girl's weekend with a bottle or two of wine."

"I can't. I, um…have plans I can't break."

One thing I had noticed since my thirtieth birthday was that my senses were heightened, and I don't only mean the five senses we're taught about in elementary school. I mentioned before that there are some things that I just *know*. And that tingling sensation was screaming at me that my mother had actual plans—like, with a man.

"Mom, are you going out on a *date*?"

"It's not a *date*, per se," my mother protested with a bit too much force. "I'm meeting someone for lunch on Saturday."

"So…a lunch date."

"Lunch."

"Lunch is food, therefore a date."

The bell above the glass door chimed, indicating my first customer of the day. I didn't have to turn around to know that it was Pearl Saffron. The woman was seventy-five years old and totally head over heels in love with Henry Wiegand. One of my Nan's love potions made sure that Henry was inclined to feel the same.

"Tell Pearl I said hello," Regina said, stunning me to the point that I didn't continue to argue about the definition of a date. How had my mother known Pearl had entered the shop? I pulled the phone away to look at the display, though that didn't give me the answers I was seeking, either. I now had a million and one questions about how she'd known who'd entered the shop's door, as well as who my mother was meeting up with—such as his name, what he looked like, his age, and what he did for a living. I had more queries, but you get the gist. "And it's not a date."

My mother had a tendency to try and always get the last word. She won this round, because there was nothing I could do about her cutting off our connection.

"Raven, dear," Pearl greeted in a sing-song, her overpowering perfume giving me the sudden urge to clear my throat. "How are you this morning?"

"I'm good, Pearl." I tossed a smile over my shoulder before walking to the counter and storing my cell phone in the small cubby underneath the cash register. "How is Henry doing?"

"Wonderfully," Pearl gushed, patting the back of her hair…which was, of all colors, purple. I'd asked Candy, who owned the local hair salon, about the vivid hue once. Turns out, Pearl thought it was a bright silver and no one could convince her otherwise. "He's across the street getting us a booth over at the diner for breakfast."

I had learned the most important element of any love spell during my initial training sessions with Leo. The magic couldn't work if the person on the receiving end didn't have some sort of romantic leanings toward the intended person indicated by the spell. The magic just facilitated the process. The person for whom the spell was created for became enlightened toward discovering their feelings. The target of those affections tasted a sweet fruity sensation on their tongue. A kinship was then formed that each of them experienced.

It's silly, I know, but it made me feel better knowing that I wasn't forcing someone to reciprocate love for another whom they didn't truly have those feelings for.

"What can I get for you today?" I hadn't seen a lot of Pearl in the last couple of weeks, but that was due to the fact that she no longer needed the tea blends for Henry. The initial discovery had been enough to ignite the spark that was needed. The magic used had been successful. "I'm out of the pumpkin spiced chai tea, but I do have—"

"I don't need *that* kind of tea," Pearl whispered, lowering her head and raising her eyebrows. I found myself almost mimicking her motions in my attempt to understand her. "I have a bit of a…problem."

I couldn't help but sigh in despair now that I'd figured out where this conversation was going. You see, Pearl was the initial reason I thought Nan had been a legit drug dealer.

Seriously.

I'm not kidding.

I'd even marched myself over to the diner to confess everything to Liam. Turns out, the residents believed it was Pearl who was a little crazy in the noggin. She believed that Nan truly was a witch, with magic spells and the whole lot without the pointy hat.

I suppose I should have been grateful to her, but it also made the situation awkward when Pearl treated me like her own little spell machine cranking out her desired remedies.

I still played along.

"What's happened now?" I asked, leaning over the counter as

if we were conspiring against the natural order of things. "Does Henry not want to stay in town for Christmas?"

The last time I'd seen Pearl was Wednesday, when she'd come into the shop claiming she needed a hex bag to prevent Henry from going to Florida to spend time at his winter residence. I'd had her order ready by Friday, and Wilma and Elsie had informed me yesterday that Henry decided to postpone his trip until January.

See?

I didn't always catch my blouse on fire.

"There are rumors that the reason Cora Barnes looks so young is that she's drinking some of your special tea blends," Pearl whispered, glancing over her shoulder to make sure no one walked into the shop without her seeing. I didn't bother to remind her that there was a bell overhead for that exact reason. "I was hoping you could make me some of that tea, just as a precaution against the ravages of time."

Tell her the truth. It won't work at her age. I mean, have you seen those wrinkles?

Leave it to Leo to make such a grand entrance.

"Pearl, do you truly believe that Henry doesn't think you're beautiful as you are?" I'd discovered that being a witch was also like being a psychologist. Listen to your patient, diagnose what he or she needs, and then write him or her a prescription. But sometimes all that was required was listening. "Look at you. What is your skin care regime, anyway? Honestly, I need some of that stuff for myself. You've got impeccable taste, you never have a strand of hair out of place, and your choice of attire is just stunning."

Pearl was beaming by the time I'd gotten done pointing out her finer attributes. Sure, she fought with insecurity and loneliness. Didn't we all?

Speak for yourself. I rock this body like it's 1999.

I couldn't help but look over to where Leo was strolling this way, his head held high as he swayed his bent tail back and forth. He'd originally hated the tufts of fur on his body, his kinked tail, and crooked whiskers. The thing of it was, he had changed his opinion about his disheveled appearance after Heidi began fawning all over him.

I was pretty sure Leo had a secret crush on Heidi.

I do not.

"Henry did say I was beautiful this morning," Pearl crooned, her cheeks flushing with excitement. "I guess I'll just take some English Breakfast blend then."

"Coming right up."

I loved days like this, where the customers bought the regular inventory and there was no need to add a sprinkle of magical components that I'd need to harvest. Let me tell you, it certainly wasn't easy learning all those specific spells with their material, semantic, and verbal pieces. I might have touched on a few dozen out of a thousand possible variants, with maybe eight of them being completely successful.

More like a few hundred thousand magical possibilities with seven turning out somewhat decent thus far, but who's counting?

"I had an appointment with Candy yesterday afternoon, and she told me what happened at the inn." Pearl was twirling the opal on her necklace, pretending that she didn't want a firsthand account of the events. I smothered a groan of irritation. "Can you believe that those people are actually going to go through with the audit? I can only imagine that Oliver is fit to be tied."

"Why does everyone assume that Oliver is upset over this audit?" I asked, thinking maybe I was missing something. "From my understanding, audits of this type are routine."

You could always ask the sheriff on your date…that you should most certainly cancel.

I disregarded Leo as I sealed the paper bag I'd filled with English Breakfast tea leaves that I'd weighed carefully on the scale. It took me only seconds to peel off one of the gold stickers I'd printed up with fonts similar to the shop's name hand-painted on the display window. The quaint addition to my marketing plan had been getting a lot of compliments.

Who are you kidding? You saw it on Pinterest. Theft of intellectual property is a crime.

Leo had a tendency to rain on my parades, so I went back to ignoring him.

"Oh, Oliver and Ben Stanway go way back," Pearl shared with a bit of excitement, having realized I didn't know the entire story. I wasn't sure I wanted to hear any of it. "Technically, Ben and the former sheriff go way back. Did you not know that Otis and Ben had been fishing buddies?"

No, I hadn't known that. No wonder Detective Swanson had asked Liam to reach out to Otis.

Oh, wait. It's beginning to come back to me.

I shot Leo an infuriating glance.

"Anyway, Otis supposedly told Ben that he might want to look into the town's finances one day. Oliver took offense to that, of course. Otis said it originally in jest, of course, considering the funds had seen a tidy profit. You know how those old fools can be when they hit the tavern." Peal was too busy pulling out her wallet to notice that she basically had me spellbound with her story. It had me wondering if Oliver really did have something to do with Mr. Stanway's murder. "Oliver didn't appreciate someone suggesting that the funds had been tampered with by the new firm. He took it personally, and he didn't find the claim funny in the least. He certainly didn't consider it a laughing matter, which then started the rumors that maybe he had tampered with the town's finances."

Nope. I've lost it.

Leo's whiskers twitched to show his displeasure as he strolled past Pearl to his favorite resting spot—his pillow in the display window.

Pearl took too long to explain. She's long-winded for an old biddy, isn't she?

"What was the outcome?" I asked, taking the twenty-dollar bill the elderly woman had handed over. I gave my new credit card machine a forlorn glance, hoping one day it would finally get some use. "And do you know if Mr. Stanway ever stopped in here at the shop when Nan was here?"

Are you trying to open a can of worms on purpose? You know, it's possible to fish without them.

"Well, I assume everything was just fine when Ben came back that following fall to go fishing with Otis as if nothing had happened." Pearl took the change I'd gotten out of the cash register, carefully sliding the individual dollar bills inside her wallet in her typical deliberate way. I couldn't help but wonder if the arthritis blend that Otis came in for wouldn't benefit Pearl's joints. Her knuckles were awfully swollen. "Now that I think about it, nothing was ever said one way or another. As for whether or not Ben visited *Tea, Leaves, & Eves*…well, I wouldn't be surprised if he'd stopped in with Otis. This shop is quite the attraction with all the herbal remedy blends you have in here."

Pearl winked at me as if we had our own little secret. Why my Nan had chosen a select handful of individuals to sell bewitching potions and blends to, I will never know.

Pearl is harmless. No one believed her whispers of Rosemary being a witch, just as they won't with you.

I still believed Nan had been taking a chance with her secret, but what was done was done. I'd do my best from here on out to stick to the so-called herbal remedies. Which reminded me that Otis stopped in every Friday morning for the special tea blend I'd learned to make. As a matter of fact, it was the first spell I'd perfected.

After you made my tail go numb…twice.

"Ted stepped on your tail the first time. It had nothing to do with—" I realized my mistake too late, so I had no choice but to improvise. "Oh, Pearl. How silly of me. I just saw Leo licking his tail. He'll be fine, but you can imagine how bad that hurt considering Ted's size."

"How is Ted?" Pearl asked fondly, having already stored her wallet back in her purse. My cover seemed to work, and she now cradled the tea leaves she'd purchased in her hand. "I always thought it was so nice of your grandmother to let him stay with her on the property. I mean, that's what we all do for family, right?"

Pearl reminded me of Gertie in that both women were rather spritely. They could move with speed in an unexpected manner, which was why I didn't get to ask any follow up questions about Ted being related to Nan. I'm pretty sure that wasn't the case at all.

"I better join Henry over at the diner before he comes looking for me. Ta-ta."

I zeroed my sights on Leo.

"What did Pearl mean by Ted being family?" I asked Leo after the shop door closed. Both of us watched the purple-haired lady make her way slowly across the street. Her response had me wondering what exactly the residents thought of good ol' Ted. "Is that how Nan spun his sudden appearance…whatever she did to bring him around?"

Don't get me wrong.

Finding out I was a witch pretty much had me believing I'd lost my mind. I mean, complete insanity wasn't beyond the possibilities here. And I'm not talking about me missing my morning coffee, either.

Accepting my lot in life, as well as my lineage, was made even harder due to my mother wanting me to leave it all behind and forget. I guess what I'm trying to say is that I'm not so sure other…beings…might actually exist.

Could there be vampires, werewolves, or some kind of—

What do you think this is? A Saturday morning television show?

"I'm talking to a cat that was brought back from the dead," I replied wryly, about to turn away from the view of the main drag when something caught my attention. Well, more like a couple of someones. "Isn't that…"

Sure enough, Rachel Duggan and Valerie Jacoba were walking down the sidewalk on the opposite side of the street toward the diner. Leo was staring in their direction, and I could sense the tension in the air begin to simmer slightly at his observation.

"The one in the white dress coat is Rachel Duggan. The other one bundled up in the scarf is Valerie Jacoba." Leo had a way of knowing things, but I always liked to make sure we were on the same page. "Oh, shoot. I think they're headed this way."

Does she think we live in Antarctica?

It didn't take a genius to figure out that Leo was talking about Valerie. I didn't get a chance to speak with the woman personally yesterday, but that wasn't strange after what had happened to Ben Stanway.

Look at what you've done. They're heading over here. What did you say to them yesterday?

"I didn't say anything to them." Defending myself against any of Leo's claims were useless, but I could never seem to stop myself. "Don't you find it odd that Rachel wears white this late in the year?"

That's what you're thinking about right now, of all things?

Leo was starting to get worked up again, but I honestly didn't believe we had anything to be concerned about. I mean, I sell tea. They probably saw the shop and decided to stop in before having breakfast at the diner. Maybe they were being nice and checking up on me, considering I'd been at the scene of the crime with them.

You're a New Yorker. I know you're not that naïve. Get a grip. And doesn't the inn serve them a free breakfast?

The duo finally managed to cross the street and was at the door before I could respond to Leo's inquiry.

"Good morning," I greeted, pasting a caring smile on my face. All I saw when looking at Rachel was the memory of her running down the stairs. One couldn't fake that kind of frightened response, right? "How are you two doing after yesterday?"

"We're managing." The tips of Rachel's ears were red from the bitter cold, as was her nose. Or was that from crying? "Have you heard anything? Detective Swanson hasn't been back to the inn to let us know anything."

"I haven't," I reluctantly replied, wishing I had some answers for them. I stepped forward and held out my hand to Valerie. "We haven't properly met. I'm Raven Marigold."

Valerie's eyes filled with tears, but she took off her knitted mitten and returned my gesture. She wasn't as stylish as Rachel, by any means. There was no flashy jewelry or designer clothes, but she didn't need all of that. I recalled from yesterday that she was a dishwater blonde, not that I could see her hair underneath her hat at the moment.

"Isn't it just awful?" Valerie said, wiping her nose discreetly with the mitten. The inconspicuous act was actually quite disgusting. "Ben might not have been the easiest man to work with, but no one deserves to be stabbed to death like that."

You might want to wash your hands.

I somehow managed to catch myself before shooting Leo a dirty look.

"Had Mr. Stanway severely upset someone recently?" I really shouldn't be asking these kinds of questions, but I was still trying to figure out why he would have bought a protection spell from my grandmother. It seemed reasonable to conclude that whoever he was afraid of had actually succeeded in finishing the job. Did that mean the spell hadn't worked? "I can imagine that being an auditor doesn't make it easy to have too many friends."

How dare you question Rosemary's spells? The woman was a witch goddess. Besides, it's obvious that he hasn't been back here since her passing. I'm sure he ran out of whatever tea blend she'd whipped up, leaving him vulnerable. An unfortunate fate, indeed.

"If you ask me, I think the wife paid someone knock him off," Rachel said with a lot more composure than she'd had yesterday. And a bit snippy, if you ask me. "Ben continuously complained about their marriage."

It's always the spouse.

It would make sense. Though that didn't explain how Ben knew of Nan's ability to create such spells. Otis used the tea shop's side business to help ease his arthritis. He didn't know that Nan added a bit of magic to the mix, making it the best remedy he'd ever found.

Otis probably told him about Pearl and Henry. Oh, and don't forget about Cora. I mean, do I have to mention wrinkles again? That would make anyone believe in magic.

I was about to reply that Henry had more wrinkles than Pearl, but it didn't matter what either one of them looked like. Pearl was beautiful the way she was, and Henry was rather distinguished for an eighty-six-year-old man. As for Cora, well, she had benefited beautifully from the ageing enchantment. Only time would tell what would become of her smooth features the longer she didn't drink the bewitching blend now that I'd stopped making it for her.

And who was Leo to talk about looks, anyway?

My whiskers are growing on me.

"Rachel's right," Valerie reluctantly agreed, removing her other mitten. The shop was kept at a very comfortable temperature of seventy-two degrees, so I can imagine she was getting somewhat warm standing in the middle of the store bundled up like she was ready to go ice-fishing. "Natalie isn't that nice to anyone, but no one else was at the inn. Not unless someone snuck inside, up the stairs, and knew what room Ben occupied."

"Wouldn't Natalie have information on Ben's reservation?" Rachel pointed out, flicking away what had to be an imaginary piece of lint. The fabric on her coat was pristine. "Anyway, we thought we'd stop into the police station before going to Mr. Bend's office. We were hoping he had some news for us, but it's looking as if we might be able to give him some information about Natalie Stanway. Would you like to come with us?"

Oh, these two could take over for the sheriff. That would solve all our problems.

"No, thank you," I responded, telling myself it was better

that I not get involved in another murder since I'd only been in town for a couple months.

I'd already seen and done enough.

Exactly. Let them talk to the sheriff and solve our problem. Maybe it will keep him busy for a while running around and chasing their suspicions.

We didn't have a problem. Leo had a problem, and he would just have to get over it. I was going on that date just like I'd agreed, and nothing was going to stop me.

Chapter Six

*A*RE YOU SURE *you want to do this now?*

"Yes," I answered for the hundredth time. I'd changed my mind about waiting to speak with Gertie. "I'm not ordering such a large supply of specialty tea blends without verifying the amount and specific selections with Gertie first."

And it has nothing to do with the fact that it's dinnertime and every guest is probably gathered in the dining room enjoying their meal?

Leo and I were currently walking down the sidewalk of River Bay. The occasional flurry was floating softly to the ground from a rather overcast evening. Signs for various storefronts were being flipped over to signify that they were closing for the day, and the streetlights had already popped on overhead.

The crews had come through earlier during the day to hang the Christmas decorations from the lampposts. The new holiday pennants were adorned with jolly snowmen, Santa's elves, red-nosed reindeer, and presents wrapped in colorful bows.

The townsfolk, together with the local merchants, had invested in the more traditional holiday theme. Each of the festive depictions were high up on the posts, centered inside a fresh Christmas wreath with every color of bulb imaginable. The length of the lanyard from which it was hung was draped with dark green garland and more colorful lights.

The Christmas season had truly arrived in Paramour Bay.

Unfortunately, there was another thing that was hard not to notice.

The palm of my hand became warmer the closer I got to reaching the inn. It occurred to me that there was one way to have Leo stop nagging me about my plans, but it could backfire. Maybe I would finally get some answers if I rattled his cage.

A gust of wind hit me in the face, causing me to lift my scarf a bit higher. It was better that way, because no one would think I was losing my marbles as I had a conversation with my cat. We must look like quite the pair walking side by side down the sidewalk.

"Remember when you said that we would discuss the heat in my hand? It's been coming and going ever since Halloween night. We never did talk about it, but you should know that I'm feeling something in my fingers now, too." I wiggled the tips of my right glove. "The sensation is similar to when a static electricity charge begins to build."

We should turn back. Aren't you hungry? I'm hungry.

"Why have you been avoiding this conversation?" I'd originally brought up the subject of my hand to avoid being lectured about visiting Gertie, but Leo's ever-present evasion on some of my recent questions was becoming rather annoying. "Leo, haven't I already proved that I can handle this whole witchcraft thing?"

I'll believe you're ready when you stop calling it a thing.

"And what if you forget by then? Let's face it, your short-term memory loss is a critical factor that we're dealing with here." I waited for the standard witty reply, but I was only greeted with silence. "Leo?"

Sure enough, Leo was no longer by my side. He'd probably

gotten distracted by a blowing leaf or something equally inane. There were times I wish I had the ability to appear and disappear at will. It wasn't fair that he was keeping secrets from me, but we'd have to have another sober discussion very soon.

It took me a little longer to reach the inn given the cold gusts of winds and the lack of urgency in my step. It made me question if it was a wise idea to walk instead of drive, but the inn was only a couple of blocks away from the tea shop. Besides, I still had to place my weekly order on top of my nightly studies.

I couldn't help but glance up at the old Victorian home as I began my ascent on the worn cement steps. Architects no longer made homes like these, opting for cheaper materials that would eventually need to be replaced. Everything seemed to be about money these days.

Gertie must have employed an army of seasonal workers to decorate the old place.

Garland and large red bows beautified the railings. In each window stood a single candle in a vintage metal and glass lantern burning brightly, denoting the hospitality of the season and the welcoming warmth within. Jack Frost put the finishing touches on the plate glass windows, etching his best artistic effort on each and every pane. I was eager to partake of that promised warmth.

I could have contemplated the hypocrisy of my seasonal opinion, considering I was here to sell tea leaves, but the slight movement of a curtain in an upstairs window caught my eye. I couldn't help but glance back, trying to make out the identity of the person peering out at me.

A sharp prick in my finger had me turning away.

Ouch!

That hurt.

I rubbed the tip of my middle finger through my glove,

eventually getting the piercing pain to fade. By the time I looked back at the window, the curtain had shifted into place as if it had never been moved at all.

As I slowly closed the distance to the front door, I couldn't help but think about my conversation with Rachel and Valerie that very morning. Were they right? Had Natalie Stanway sent some clandestine killer to Paramour Bay to murder her husband?

I'm not sure when you became an amateur detective, but you're going to get us all killed one day.

I'm pretty sure the soles of my knee-high boots came off the porch a couple of inches as Leo's voice reverberated through my head.

"You're as bad as Ted lately!" I admonished in a harsh whisper, unable to stop myself from stomping my foot in agitation. "Stop sneaking up on me, Leo."

I didn't give him time to say anything as I lifted the heavy brass knocker and banged it a couple of times to let Gertie know she had a new arrival. I could have most likely just walked right in, considering it was a B&B, but it paid to have manners in a small town.

Is that how the killer gained access to Ben Stanway's room?

Did he or she just walk right through the door to the inn as if they were a guest?

I'm going to start calling you Nancy.

"Raven!" Gertie exclaimed, using her cane to shuffle backward a step. I wasn't surprised it was she who answered the manor's main door. I'd been standing on the doorstep for close to a minute, and my cheeks had become somewhat numb from the crosswinds on the porch. "What a welcome surprise. Come in, come in. It's awfully cold out there, dear."

"Thanks, Gertie."

I stepped across the threshold and into a blanket of warmth. The air in the entryway smelled of that sweet fragrance that had hung in the air yesterday. It was similar to my favorite scent of salted caramel in those Yankee Candles I loved so much.

To one side of me was the sturdy oak coat rack draped with the guests' jackets, and to the other was an antique Edwardian entry table covered with candy dishes and plates of sugar cookies iced to look like poinsettias.

My stomach growled a bit to remind me I hadn't had dinner.

A small shudder went through me that had nothing to do with my hunger or the instant temperature change.

You see, every single guest was seated on those couches I'd admired on my last visit.

Everyone.

I counted them twice.

So, who had been upstairs?

The entry immediately opened into the front sitting room with the stairs to the upper levels just twelve feet to my left. The dining room, which was through a large archway and past the sitting area, appeared empty. Everyone was gathered in front of the fire for coffee and tea…English-style tea.

"I don't want to keep you, Gertie, but I filled out your order form. I know you said it was okay to choose for you, but I just didn't feel comfortable doing that yet since this is our first season together."

"Aren't you a dear?" Gertie was able to close the door after I'd moved out of the way. She gestured that I should take my coat off. "Come into the kitchen with me, dear. I was just putting the finishing touches on dinner."

I couldn't imagine Gertie having enough energy to cook for

herself, let alone a houseful of guests. Maybe Kimmie was in the kitchen helping out, though I couldn't imagine someone so young working so many hours. Then again, hadn't I done the same at twenty years of age?

Rachel and Valerie gave me a small gesture of a wave, but the two men had their heads down over what appeared to be reports of some sort. They were in their own little world and hadn't noticed that someone new had entered the room. From my understanding, no one else was staying at the inn other than the auditors.

Had whoever been in the upstairs window made it downstairs before I'd stepped through the front door?

"I don't want to be a bother, Gertie." I didn't remove my coat, but I did loosen the scarf around my neck so that I could breathe a little easier. As I removed my gloves, I noticed the heat in my hand still remained. "I just need a moment of your time to sign off on the order."

"Don't be silly." Gertie lifted her cane to gesture toward the kitchen. "Have you eaten? Beverly has made the most wonderful chicken marsala for our guests, along with the appropriate side dishes, of course. We have peach cobbler for dessert tonight. You can't miss out on warm cobbler with a scoop of French vanilla ice cream on the side."

Beverly? As in Beverly Garber?

I'm pretty sure she was in the ladies' auxiliary with Cora Barnes. If you recall, Cora certainly wasn't a fan of me or my mother at our first meeting. Technically, I'm pretty sure she hadn't liked any of the Marigolds from what I gathered. The only reason she had been nice to Nan was because of the aging spell she'd continued to pay for over the years, which I'll have you know I haven't quite perfected yet.

At the rate I was going on that spell, she could end up looking like a sow's ear if she relied on me to supply her needs.

Of course, the entire group of ladies thought it was an herbal remedy that my Nan had somehow discovered that thousands of scientists and doctors hadn't managed to uncover over the course of many lifetime's worth of research.

If only they knew...

Anyway, I doubt that Beverly was a fan of mine. It was too late to come up with an excuse as to why I couldn't stay. Gertie had already made it halfway across the front room. Was it bad of me to think that she could have killed Ben Stanway? After all, she technically hadn't been within eyesight when the body was discovered.

But when *had* the murder occurred exactly?

It could have been when Kimmie hadn't been in the kitchen while attending to her other chores. Could a twenty-year-old have the audacity to murder someone in cold blood?

Oh, this was bad.

Was Leo right?

Did I now think of myself as some amateur gumshoe who could solve murders?

I certainly didn't want to go down that road, especially given all that I was dealing with these last couple of months. We all needed Paramour Bay to go back to normal, back before my Nan dropped dead of a heart attack on her daily walk and the rash of recent murders. Don't think it hadn't occurred to me that her death hadn't been of natural causes, but there was no evidence to the contrary.

What did strike me out of the blue was the fact that I could technically help solve this murder mystery. Nan had made money from her side business in the name of helping others, so why couldn't I do the same?

Sure, it was in a completely different manner than providing herbal remedies. But using divination to assist in an investigation was still considered helping others, right? Liam or Detective Swanson didn't need to know how I came about certain information. I was proud of my rationalization skills. I could definitely pull that off.

"Raven?"

I'd gotten myself all worked up, not realizing that Gertie had been waiting on me the entire time I was standing there lollygagging. That was a word my mother used when I was younger and prone to daydreaming. It had stuck with me ever since. The auditors didn't seem too enthusiastic that I'd been staring at them, but I'm sure I was the least of their worries.

It was probably a good thing Leo wasn't inside the manor with me. He might have clawed his own whiskers out had he discovered that I'd figured out a way to help solve this murder.

"Sorry," I called out, not bothering to take my boots off in the foyer once I realized that no one else had done so. Giving it some thought, I guess one didn't take their shoes off in a hotel. That's what a B&B was, technically. "I'm right behind you, Gertie."

The delicious aroma of baked chicken and tangy tomato sauce became stronger the closer I got to the kitchen. My stomach rumbled, reminding me once again that I had yet to eat dinner. I usually ate around seven o'clock when I got home from the shop, but my light lunch obviously hadn't kept up with my busy schedule.

"Beverly, have you met Raven Marigold?" Gertie walked over to the stove to check on the progress of dinner. "Oh, this smells heavenly! You've outdone yourself yet again, Bev."

"It's nice to meet you, Mrs. Garber." I didn't bother to hold my hand out, seeing that the other woman was busy dishing out breaded chicken breasts onto cooked pasta that had already been served onto beautiful china. "I didn't realize that you worked for Gertie."

"Oh, my heavens," Beverly exclaimed, seemingly not holding the grudge that I'd thought would be there courtesy of Cora Barnes. "I've been with Gertie for over thirty years. Kimmie handles breakfast and lunch, while I cook dinner, clean the rooms, and do the linens—among other things. It's nice to finally meet the infamous granddaughter of Rosemary Marigold. I was wondering when I'd get the opportunity."

Infamous?

I held back a laugh as I pulled out the file I'd put together for Gertie from my purse. My palm was no longer warm, and the aura in the air from Beverly's presence told me that she was a good person after all.

Did that mean everyone in the living room had ill intentions?

No, that couldn't be right.

But it could mean that one of them was the individual responsible for killing Ben Stanway. That had a better chance of being true.

Leo was always telling me that my new powers connected me to the earth. Therefore, it seemed to reason that my intuitive nature was right on point, whether by supernatural means or just good old common sense. I'd know more about the heat in my hand if only Leo would take two seconds to give me a straight answer.

"It's nice to meet you, as well," I replied sincerely, taking a seat at the kitchen table while I waited for Gertie to make her way back to me. "I'll be honest. I wasn't sure what kind of reception I would get, seeing as you are friends with Cora. In case you weren't aware, she's not my biggest fan."

"Oh, now don't you go worrying about Cora Barnes and all her nonsense," Beverly dismissed with a wave of her hand. She finished her job by laying a piece of parsley on top of each breaded chicken breast. I could also smell a dash of garlic, so it wasn't surprising when she added a basket of toasted French bread to one of the trays. "Sit and chat with Gertie while I take these meals out to those auditor folks and announce dinner. She's been a bit shaky ever since yesterday."

I stood up and pulled out a chair for Gertie. She slowly made her way over to the table and hung her cane on the back of the seat. Once she was settled, I joined her and slid the folder closer to her side so that she didn't have to reach for it.

We spent a few minutes going over what flavors of tea I believed her guests might enjoy throughout the winter. I was more comfortable with implementing a six-month supply of tea rather than an annual one, just due to the freshness of the tea leaves and availability of certain blends during the year.

"This is perfect, Raven," Gertie gushed, signing her name with trembling hands. I almost suggested that she personally try the tea blend I made for Otis that included the pain relief spell, but it was probably best I bring that up at another time. "When do you expect enough inventory to arrive to fill my order? Ms. Duggan is a tea drinker, as well as Mr. Edlyn."

"I can be back in the morning with what I have on hand, and I'll have the other half to you by next week at the latest." I gathered up the paperwork and slipped it back into the folder. A jolt of excitement shot through me at completing my first large order for a small business. "Does that sound good to you?"

"Yes, dear," Gertie replied, patting me on the shoulder before she slowly managed to stand. "Would you like to stay for dinner?"

"Oh no, thank you. I still have a few pressing matters at the shop." A part of me really wanted to take Gertie up on her offer. After all, it would be a way for me to get to know the guests. I first needed to run a few things past Leo, the most important being the use of a certain type of witchcraft to solve Ben Stanway's murder. I personally thought it was a fantastic idea. "I should be heading home. I'm sure Leo is getting hungry, and you know how cats can be when they don't get their way on their time schedule."

It was a good thing Leo wasn't here to hear me say that. Speaking of things that didn't seem to be public knowledge…

"Gertie, I heard something quite strange today."

"And what is that, dear?"

"Did you know that Ben and Otis used to go fishing together? That they were friends?"

Judging from the way Gertie didn't react in surprise, I wasn't telling her anything she didn't already know.

"Why do you think Oliver practically ran Otis out of office?" Gertie shook her head in disappointment. She let one hand rest on the table, while using the other one to use her finger in order to make her point. "Don't get me wrong, I love Kimmie and Alison. Kimmie has helped out around here since she could rub two fingers together. Hospitality comes easily to her. That doesn't mean I'm a fan of Oliver Bend in any way, shape, or form."

"I didn't know that Otis resigned as sheriff because he felt pressured to do so by Oliver." I wondered if Detective Swanson was privy to that piece of information. Was that why he'd wanted Liam to contact Otis? Was the former sheriff a suspect? "How are you doing? Is there anything I can do for you?"

Before Gertie could answer, Beverly came back into the kitchen looking a bit pale. At first, I thought it was the lighting. Then she dropped a bombshell that had Gertie sitting back down in her chair with a thud.

"I think we need to call Detective Swanson," Beverly whispered before looking back over her shoulder to make sure that no one could hear her. "Mr. Edlyn just admitted to Ms. Duggan that he had a violent argument with Mr. Stanway the night before he died."

Okay.

I admit that little tidbit was probably something Detective Swanson should know, but colleagues had disagreements all the time—even determined arguments. I know I sure did when I worked as a receptionist in New York City. Some people just couldn't see reason.

Beverly wasn't done sharing, though.

And what she had to say next was a doozy.

Maybe I wouldn't need to use magic on this case, after all.

"Mr. Edlyn was taking bribes from Oliver, and Mr. Stanway found out and threatened to expose him." Beverly rested a trembling hand over her heart, though her tremors had nothing to do with old age and everything to do with shock. "I think Mr. Edlyn is the murderer!"

Chapter Seven

"USING MAGIC TO help solve a murder is the same thing as me helping Wilma get rid of her cold," I argued, wishing Leo would see the reasoning behind my argument. "We can do this Leo. Together. I'll have you know that Wilma stopped into the shop this morning without so much as a sniffle in her little head."

Did you forget that you caught yourself on fire last week doing some rather mundane spell work? Or that you couldn't sleep a wink two nights ago? Let's not forget that I wasn't able to feel my tail for nearly four hours after you tried out that spell to help Otis with his arthritis.

"Hey, I ended up perfecting that spell."

I was sitting on the stool behind the cash register while watching Eileen lock up the sheriff's station. The town's dispatcher was pretty chatty once someone got her going, and I contemplated going outside to see if she had any information about what Beverly had overheard last night. The sudden gust of wind that practically knocked the woman on her butt changed my mind about venturing out.

I quickly averted my gaze to the spell book splayed out in front of me. It was only five-thirty in the evening, but it was already dark outside. Eileen only had to look across the street to catch me watching her.

"I learned pretty quick what happens when the wrong ingredients are added together. I won't do that again." I tapped the feathered pen against the counter as I thought through what I could accomplish for this town if only my learning curve wasn't so...stunted. "I'm closing up, and you're going to teach me another spell."

Not here, we're not.

"Fine. We'll head home first."

I stood from the stool and smoothed out my skirt. I was wearing a soft peacock green turtleneck that I'd bought in Mindy's boutique. She had some really cute things for sale, but I was being very careful with my finances until I figured out what I had to play with.

Did you send that rent check to your landlord?

"Previous landlord," I responded wryly, hating when Leo reminded me that I had been pretty much broke before moving to Paramour Bay. "And yes, I did. I'm not the one with short term memory loss, remember?"

I smiled when my wittiness earned me a sideways glance from those green slits of his.

You still haven't mastered the hair growth. You told Candy that it would be ready in time for the Christmas rush.

I had promised Candy that I would have the tea blend ready for next week, but wasn't solving a murder more important?

"If you help me like you're supposed to, I'll be able to do both of them tonight."

Uh-oh.

"What do you mean uh-oh?" I had been in the midst of collecting my things when Leo's warning stopped me in my tracks. "Leo?"

I turned around to see what had caught his attention.

Isn't that one of the auditors?

"Is someone walking this way?" I stood frozen as I observed Neal Edlyn crossing the street. Eileen was sitting in her vehicle, most likely waiting for the engine to warm up. That didn't stop her from blatantly staring at Mr. Edlyn as he continued to head this way. "He *is* coming into the shop. See, Leo? I should know a spell or something that could make him confess."

Oh, stop being dramatic. Your precious sheriff told Beverly last night that Neal Edlyn hadn't done anything wrong in accepting those Cuban cigars from Oliver Bend. They were given as a gift, and not intended as a bribe or anything like that.

"Ben Stanway obviously disagreed with that assessment," I managed to get out right before Neal Edlyn reached out with a black glove to open the glass door of the tea shop. Was it bad of me to imagine that gloved hand pulling back and slashing the air as it came down and…

Did anyone ever tell you that you have a morbid imagination?

"Mr. Edlyn, it's nice to see you." I casually opened the drawer underneath the register and set Nan's spell book inside. Technically, it was mine now, but I still had trouble owning up to the possession of such an item. "I heard about all the trouble last night. I hope everything's been cleared up."

You have absolutely no couth.

I hadn't meant to say anything about Beverly's accusation after she'd overheard Mr. Edlyn talking about the argument he'd had with Ben Stanway. The New Yorker in me had other plans, but it was a way to break the ice.

What? With a stick of dynamite?

"Oh, Oliver and I go way back over the years," Neal replied with a half-smile that didn't seem all that genuine. He began to remove his gloves one finger at a time, which caused the palm of my hand to start warming up. "We attended college together, obtained our financial degrees, and even vied for the same position at a tax firm fresh after graduation. We've been through thick and thin together."

"I'm surprised that you're allowed to be on the team of auditors, considering that fact." Once again, the words came out a lot different than what they'd sounded like in my head. I forced a laugh, wishing I'd flipped over the closed sign the moment I saw Eileen locking up the sheriff's office. "But what do I know? What can I help you with today?"

"Gertie serves her tea in bags." Neal had both gloves off now, which for some reason was a welcome relief. Should he try anything, he'd leave fingerprints. "As much as I appreciate the gesture and will use whatever is on hand when I'd love a cup of tea, me and my team will be here for a week or two while we complete the audit on your town's financial records."

Fingerprints? That's what you're thinking about right now? The man just wants his...did you say that your palm is warm?

Leo sometimes took a while to catch on, though those times were rare. He really was an intelligent feline, but his thinking outraced his mouth by several hundred yards. He had wisdom beyond his years and that of a human, but his choice of when to dish out that knowledge could stand to be tweaked.

"Your team?" I asked, having caught the specific way Mr. Edlyn had worded his sentence. "Have you taken over for Mr. Stanway as team leader?"

"Yes, though this wasn't how I would've wished for my promotion to happen after all my hard work." Mr. Edlyn shook his head in sorrow, even lowering his head slightly as if in prayer. I couldn't tell if he was being genuine or not. "I was hoping that I could purchase a two and a half snap ball tea infuser and three ounces of Lavender Earl Grey."

There was no doubt that this man knew his tea.

Mr. Edlyn had even walked over to where I kept a display of various tea infusers to see what I had on hand. There were quite a few made of stainless steel and a mesh material that allowed for the tea leaves to steep properly in water poured just short of the boil.

As for his particular selection of tea leaves, Lavender Earl Grey was rather strong and spicy to the unsophisticated palate. His selection also offered a high amount of caffeine compared with commonly established pedestrian afternoon blends. His was more of a high tea draft for flagging spirits late in the day.

Which means that this not-so-charming fellow actually came inside the shop to buy tea. That makes me feel better. By the way, is your palm still warm?

"I'm sorry, Mr. Edlyn, but we sell our tea leaves in four, eight, or sixteen ounces." I made sure the drawer with my spell book was closed up tight before stepping out from behind the register. "I do offer a five percent discount for first purchases, though. You'll still come out ahead by choosing the four ounces. I recently restocked two pounds of that exact blend. Do you have a tea tin for storage?"

"Oh, four is fine. I'm used to buying my tea leaves online. I do have a suitable tin to store them. And please, call me Neal." He began to slowly walk around the shop and look at all the items on display. I was very proud of myself for adding a touch of colorful lights for the holiday season, even including a sprinkle of the fake snow on the display tables to get the full effect. "I've been to Paramour Bay before, and I've always found it to be such a quaint little town. Surprisingly enough, there's quite a bit of entertainment and specialty shops to choose from."

"You must be talking about our wax museum." I had already weighed the tea leaves to the exact amount and was in the process of folding the top of the brown paper bag so that I could add my shop's logo seal to it. "It's kind of hard to miss something that unique when it's located right across the street from the inn."

"I haven't had a chance to go inside, but it's on my list of things to do this weekend. Rachel and David will most likely stay in the city for the rest of their weekend after we attend Ben's funeral." Neal had walked back to the display of tea infusers, choosing one of the pricier sterling silver models featuring a lion motif on the handle. He stared at it for quite a while, and I began to experience remorse at believing this man was a murderer. "It doesn't seem quite real."

The warmth in my hand began to dissipate, though it didn't completely fade.

Fine. I'll tell you. It's energy that builds up at any sign of danger. It's your body's way of protecting you. You need to harness that energy or...

"Or what?"

Oh, that's not good. Think quick.

Neal turned on the heel of his dress shoe at the question that I'd so unwisely spat out to Leo. I know I must have looked like a doe caught in the headlights of a vehicle, but my mind was racing with ways to cover up my odd behavior.

"I said that it doesn't seem real," Neal explained once more, causing me to realize he thought I hadn't heard him the first time. "Ben and I might have had our differences, but I still considered him a close friend."

I did my best not to sag in relief.

"I can only imagine how hard it is for you and the others to continue working without him there by your side." I slapped one of the shop's gold stickers on the bag to seal it in order to maintain a bit of normalcy. "Rachel and Valerie stopped in the shop yesterday morning and mentioned that Ben had a wife. Do you know her well? How is she holding up?"

I began my trek across the floor in order to ring up his purchases, but he stepped right in front of me to block my path.

It was as if a spike of fire had pierced my hand.

Breathe! Breathe! Oh, this isn't good. I didn't realize it was this bad. Why didn't you tell me? You could have hurt someone and...

Leo rambled on, but I'd taken his advice and evened out my breathing. Ever so gradually, my body began to relax.

"What were Rachel and Valerie doing here yesterday?" Neal's tone wasn't threatening, but it was clear he was confused at the information I had just shared. "I know Rachel drinks tea, but she's not a connoisseur like myself. She prefers store bought tea bags over steeping the leaves to get the perfect experience."

"I assume that Rachel and Valerie were checking in on me after being questioned by the police." I nodded in an attempt to let him know that he should let me pass. I breathed a sigh of relief when he took a step to the left. "It was nice of them to think of me, considering the circumstances."

"Of course, of course," Neal said somewhat distractedly as he came up to the counter. He laid his gloves down next to the box that contained the tea infuser. I scanned the barcode since it was in plain sight before using my cheat sheet for the tea leaves and totaled his purchases. He retrieved his wallet and much to my delight...he pulled out a credit card. "I see you take credit cards. I found out the hard way that the diner is cash only. I usually eat my meals at the inn since it's included in the nightly rate, but I do like the occasional slice of fresh pie that Trixie's Diner keeps on hand. Did you know that they're all homemade from her own mother's recipe book?"

We continued to make small talk as he swiped his credit card in the black machine I'd truly never thought would get used. It worked like a dream, and soon I was handing over the receipt that had printed out from the accompanying paper tape holder.

"Well, I best get going before the folks roll up the sidewalks around here." Neal took the bag I'd put his items in to make them easier to carry on his way back to the inn when he asked me a question I thought I'd heard wrong. "Would you care to join me for dinner tonight? We could enjoy some tea with our meal."

You heard that right. The man just asked you out on a date. What does your hand say?

"Um, I…"

In New York, I was asked out all the time. I'm a thirty-year-old woman with long black hair, green eyes, and an hourglass figure. A man's interest wasn't all that uncommon. I blamed my heritage for my somewhat shapely frame, but that didn't mean I looked like one of those witches with the wart on the end of her nose.

I'd fended off requests that weren't wanted and accepted those that held a little promise. Most hadn't turned out so good or otherwise I wouldn't be single right now. I had pretty good instincts on when the possibilities were on hand—and my previous instincts had nothing to do with the palm of my hand.

Neal Edlyn?

There was absolutely no connection there whatsoever.

I was saved from answering when the bell chimed above the door. Both Neal and I turned to see who'd come into the shop after five o'clock. Mindy breezed through the doorway with a gust of bitter cold wind.

"Are the rumors true?" Mindy asked, still shaking off the flurries that had collected on her knit cap. She continued before I was able to cut her off. "Did you snag the sheriff?"

Did she just put a spin on that one popular song? No wonder Ted has a crush on her.

I cringed at the position I now found myself in, because Mindy made me look like a gold digger.

The sheriff would have to have money for that.

I would have stomped on Leo's tail had he been close enough, but instead I pasted an apologetic smile on my face and used the situation to my advantage. Did that make me a bad person?

"Neal, I'm so sorry. I'm going to have to decline your dinner invitation with regret." It was nice to know I didn't have to give a reason, considering Mindy had already painted a somewhat tarnished excuse. "I do appreciate the offer, and I hope you enjoy the tea."

You think he's going to enjoy the tea he bought from you after that catastrophe?

There didn't seem to be any hard feelings as Neal bid me goodnight, nodding in Mindy's direction as he headed for the door. Neither Mindy or I spoke a word until the glass door had closed completely. Leo, on the other hand, came back around to the previous conversation.

How is that palm of yours now that Mr. Edlyn has left?

"Were you just asked out to dinner by two different men in one week?" Mindy removed her mittens and shoved them into the pockets of her jacket. Her brown eyes were practically golden in her excitement, but all I kept doing was opening and closing my hand. My palm was no longer warm. "What is your secret, girl? Are you wearing some magical New York perfume? It took me months to get Larry to ask me out to dinner, and here you have two men begging to spend time with you."

"I think Neal just wanted more of a discount on his tea purchases," I replied lightheartedly, not wanting to make the man's proposal for a date a bigger issue than what it was. "I heard about Larry asking you out to dinner from Elsie and Wilma. And let me tell you that those ladies are thrilled for you."

You just wait until they hear about the good ol' sheriff asking you out on a date. Am I the only one who truly understands what a bad idea that is?

"It's the reason I came over here, hoping you hadn't closed up the shop yet." Mindy pulled out her phone and immediately began showing me pictures of the new inventory she'd gotten into her boutique. "I need help deciding between the red sweater and black pants or the black sweater dress with the grayish trim. If I choose the dress, I'd wear a pair of knee-high boots and tights. What do you think is more appropriate to have dinner with Larry?"

"You know that I'll always choose anything that goes with boots." I leaned over the counter to get a better look at the choice of clothes when I realized that Neal had left his leather gloves on the counter. I grabbed them up and immediately looked out the display window, but he was nowhere to be found. "Oh, shoot. Neal forgot his gloves."

Ah…that old trick. It allows him to stop back and try again, if you didn't already know.

Mindy walked over to the door and parted it slightly, clearly to see how far down the sidewalk Neal had gotten in his walk back to the inn.

"I don't see him," Mindy exclaimed before letting the door

close and exhibiting a slight shudder at the bitter cold temperature. "I bet the man drove if he was coming from Oliver Bend's office on Brook Cove."

"You're probably right," I conceded, thinking about how cold it was at nine o'clock in the morning. All of the streets in Paramour Bay were named after some body of water. I'd found it rather odd when I'd first moved here, but I'd become used to the little quirks of living in a small town. Speaking of quirks. "You know, I haven't told Ted about your date with Larry yet. It sounds terrible, but I don't want to hurt his feelings."

"Ted? Why would Ted care if I date Larry?" Mindy asked, truly baffled by my question.

Trust me, you don't want to go there.

Go where?

I realized my mistake too late, but Mindy deserved to know what I believed to be true.

I warned you...

"Mindy, Ted stops into your store to see you at least twice a week. He walks from the other end of town, and he doesn't let the cold weather deter him," I explained, wondering how on earth this woman hadn't been able to recognize the signs. "Ted practically blushes every time I bring up your name and—"

"Raven, Ted comes into the store because he's in love with..." Mindy let her voice trail off because she began to laugh, but not in a mean manner. "It's the cutest thing, but I think he's in love with one of my mannequins."

Chapter Eight

"I SHOULD BE able to talk about all of this with my best friend." My complaints fell on deaf ears as I tossed the large, fluffy burgundy pillow onto the floor in front of the coffee table. The last thing I wanted to do after Mindy's bombshell was work on spells. My distraction was likely to cause another fire. "Heidi would understand my frustrations. I think there should be an exception to the rule. You know the one—the one where no one outside of the witchcraft community can know about witches."

There's a reason for that rule.

"Why? Because you say so?" I began to wonder just how much of Leo's lessons were biased toward his beliefs and not necessarily that of rules written in stone. I set my coffee down next to my granite mortar and pestle, bowls made of white oak and ash, in addition to my cast iron cauldron that I'd set out for my next lesson. "Has anyone ever tried to tell someone about the Marigold family's lineage? Did they suddenly combust and their ashes blow away in the wind?"

"Your mother tried to once," Ted answered from his place by the window. "She didn't combust, though."

It took a minute for his words to sink in, but I should be used to bombshells like this.

Maybe I should have spiked my coffee with some of the Irish

whiskey I kept in the cupboard over the stove.

Ted had been standing there for a good ten minutes, staring out into the darkness. He'd brought me the items I needed for the spells I was going to work on this evening, which raised more questions. That's all I seemed to do…accumulate answers.

"Okay. I'm done." I plopped down on the pillow. It was for the best just in case my legs gave out in reaction to the answers either Leo or Ted gave me in the next few minutes. "What are you, Ted? I know you're not human. And where do you get all of these ingredients? I mean, these petals from flowers that aren't native to this area can't be easy to get. And these rare herbs? I tried to order them online, and I'm pretty sure I got flagged by the government for trying to buy illegal substances."

I held up my right hand when Ted finally looked my way and Leo's whiskers twitched.

"I'm not done. What happens if I don't harness this ball of energy in my palm?"

I held up my left hand to signify they still shouldn't answer yet.

"Still not done. Did Nan have anything to do with that murder case fifty-three years ago?"

There were a lot more questions I wanted answers to, but those three might take all night for Leo or Ted to answer truthfully. The duo stared at one another, and it took me a second to realize they were hoping that the other one would talk first.

"Why is it so hard to get answers from you two?"

They were saved from replying when a knock came at the door.

"Neither one of you are leaving this house until I get some answers." I pushed myself off the pillow and made my way to the door. Ted didn't get to avoid getting another reprimand. "You could have told me someone was coming to the door."

"I didn't want to," Ted replied, squaring his shoulders even more than the ramrod straight manner in which he always stood. "I think I'll retire for the evening."

Ted's aloof response could only mean that my mother was on the other side of the door. I grabbed the handle and swung open the entrance to see if I was right.

It didn't take a genius to figure that one out...nor a witch.

"Leo, watch your tone," my mother said with a leveling look that had Leo's whiskers convulsing in irritation. "Raven, another murder? Really? Don't you see that you need to come back to the city before someone figures out that we're..."

"You can't even say it, can you?" This so wasn't how I expected to spend this evening. It didn't help that Ted had waited for Regina Lattice Marigold to cross the threshold with one travel-sized suitcase clutched in her hand before he tugged on his lapels and slipped out the door with his head held high. I was definitely not getting answers from him tonight. "We're witches, Mom."

Now you've gone and done it.

Regina slammed the door behind Ted, most likely missing him by a mere inch.

"Has Leo not been doing his job? We do not say that word out loud where someone might hear."

Just a thought, but I know an easy spell that can get rid of her.

I didn't bother to remind my mother that we were over a half mile from town. She'd worked herself up into a tizzy, and I now realized I probably should have mentioned Ben Stanway's murder when we'd been on the phone.

"Mom, what are you doing here? It's only Wednesday. Did

you take time off from work?"

"Only a day. I'm here to try and talk some sense into you," Regina all but crowed, changing tactics when her mama bear's roar hadn't received the desired reaction. Honestly, it never did anymore. Not since I'd reached my teens. "I'm hoping you'll come back to the city with me in the morning. At least until this homicide investigation is over."

You know that she'll have you handcuffed to a radiator by nightfall. Do the city apartments still have those?

"I had nothing to do with Ben Stanway's death," I exclaimed, not wanting my mother to be the cause of another murder. Leo was treading on thin ice, considering Mom could hear every word he said. I walked back to where I'd set down my coffee. Now might be a good time to add something stronger. "I was only at the inn because—"

"You were there?" Regina put a manicured hand over her heart as if I'd induced cardiac arrest. My mother shot Leo a look as if he was to blame. "This is all your fault."

I'm not the one who hid Raven's lineage from her for close to thirty years. That's on you alone, sweetheart. Maybe none of this would have happened if—

"Stop!"

I hadn't meant to shout so loud, but my thunderous directive had certainly worked. I now had both of their attentions. The house seemed to close in around us as I made myself known. I took the time to take a soothing sip of coffee, ignoring the fact that my favorite beverage had gone cold.

Unfortunately, what wasn't cold was my hand.

"Mom, I'm going to say this one more time. Ben Stanway's death has no correlation to the fact that we are witches." I closed my fingers into a fist as the warmth began to fade. That was a good thing, because I didn't want to believe that my mom was a bad person. Don't get me wrong. She had her moments, but she wasn't a criminal or anything like that. Did the warmth also invade my body when I was upset? It was something I would look out for in the future. "Now that you're here, maybe you can help me figure out *who* was responsible for his murder."

"I'm sorry, what did you say?"

Even your mother thinks this is a bad idea. I hate when we agree on stuff.

"I said that I want to help Liam with the investigation." I wasn't backing down on this. "Think about it, Mom. Nan used her spell book to help others with their physical ailments. She made it so that Otis' arthritis didn't prevent him from going out in his boat to fish. She created blends for aging, pain, ailments, and a host of other problems that the residents of Paramour Bay had so that they could live healthier and happier lives. And she did all of that in the form of tea, so that no one was none the wiser."

"And what does any of what your grandmother did have to do with you getting involved with another murder? I mean seriously, Raven. You have not been using your head since my mother left the shop and this house to you."

She's not using her gift, either.

"Curse, Leo. It's a curse." My mother set her suitcase down in the middle of the floor before she very cautiously approached the coffee table where I'd set up my mini workstation. She slowly unfastened the buttons to the dress coat she was wearing. "What is all this?"

"First, what we have *is* actually a gift," I exclaimed over the two so that they didn't get lured into another argument. "Second, Leo was giving me another lesson this evening. Mom, I can use our gift to help Liam rid the evil that has arrived on this town's doorstep."

Are we in an episode of "Scooby Doo"? Do I get a snack?

"Leo, be serious for one darn second," I reprimanded, plopping myself down on the pillow. I gestured for my mom to take a seat on the couch. She'd managed to change into a pair of black slacks and a green sweater that brought out the color of her eyes before leaving the city after her grueling work day to travel all the way out to see me. We both had very long black hair, but she always wore hers up in a clip like she was one of those older characters from "Dynasty". "I'll admit to having a bit of a problem figuring out the right amount of roots, herbs, and things of that nature. It's easier when the recipe calls for a certain number of petals and such, because all I have to do is toss one or two of those into the bowl."

See what I have to deal with?

"Leo, she's just not connecting with the earth," Regina reassured him, causing me to believe that maybe I had already spiked my coffee. A quick glance at the counter didn't reveal the familiar green Jamison's bottle I sometimes added to my evening draft. Since when did Leo and my mother bond over witchcraft? "Have you tried to teach her meditation?"

Much to my amazement, the two continued to actually have a civil conversation over my magical abilities. I cautiously leaned back against the oak casement that framed the river stones of the fireplace, grateful that I'd taken the time to light a fire before I'd settled in for my next lesson.

Listening to these two go on and on about the ways to teach me to cast a spell from some of these recipes was rather enlightening.

I have paws, Regina. Paws. Not fingers. So maybe you can show her what a pinch really means, because I'm getting nowhere.

"A pinch is a pinch. How hard can that be?"

You just wait and see. I sit here night have night having to watch her throw a lump of herbs together before correcting her. And you know what she does then? A sprinkle. Who's that going to help? Ted spends half his time recovering what spell components he can from the messes she makes.

"Does she understand that there is no exact measurement? That each spell cast is from her inner energy?"

It was like I wasn't even in the room.

They were huddled together on the couch now, both of them looking over the spell book that I'd laid out in front of the bowls. My mother's coat was now behind her while Leo was to the right of her, sitting straight up so that he could view the recipes.

This was my life.

These were my mentors.

"Maybe it's time…"

Don't even go there. The entire town of Paramour Bay would be burnt to a crisp. And how would we explain that phenomenon in the middle of winter?

I had no doubt that they were talking about the warmth that was radiating through the palm of my hand.

Burnt to a crisp?

Leo had said that I needed to harness the energy. Was it a fireball? A lightning rod? Did this mean I had…awesome supernatural powers?

Look what you've done. Now she thinks she's Wonder Woman.

"What was Raven thinking in that head of hers?"

"I didn't *think* anything, Mom," I protested, not enjoying this discussion as much as when they were talking about the spell book. "Are you going to teach me a spell or what?"

"Okay," Regina said on a resigned exhale, even going so far as to roll up her sleeves. "I'll teach you a basic spell."

Leo's whiskers twitched, and I was almost afraid to say anything for fear that my mother would change her mind. She hated magic and everything that it stood for.

Don't you dare ruin this moment.

I shot Leo a glance of irritation, but I still took his advice. I set my now empty coffee mug on the mantel, not wanting it to get in the way of whatever spell my mom was about to cast.

"We should start off simple." My mom scooted forward on the cushion, gesturing for me to do the same. I shifted until I was on my knees. "We'll do a connection spell. You already have all the ingredients."

Again, I had to wonder where Ted got all the herbs, petals, and plants that weren't native to this area. The mannequin in Mindy's shop was also still weighing heavily on my mind, but I guess I would have to wait another day for those answers. I wasn't missing out on a magic lesson from the only witch I knew who was still living…my mother.

I need to mark this on the calendar, don't I?

"What's a connection spell?" I asked, trying to read the words upside down. There's usually an incantation or verbal component that goes along with every spell cast, but I didn't understand how this could help solve Ben Stanway's murder. "Wait. Are we contacting the other side?"

My thoughts raced in a thousand different directions that had nothing to do with the current problem on hand. Could I talk to Nan? Was it possible for me to contact her? Why had Leo kept this from me? Maybe then I wouldn't have had such a hard time becoming a witch. Let's face it, it wasn't easy figuring out the supernatural and all that came with it.

"Wipe that look off your face, Raven Lattice. We are *not* contacting the other side. That kind of magic should never be practiced. Ever," my mother warned me, shooting Leo a look that said this was the exact reason why she hadn't wanted her daughter involved with witchcraft. "We need to have immediate results to see if your spells are working correctly."

"My spells *are* working," I argued, a little miffed that my mom thought I wasn't capable of creating magic. "The cold remedy I cast for Wilma had her up and about the next day as if she had never been sick. And don't forget Otis' arthritis blend. It took me a long time to get that one just right."

Please don't remind me.

"I'm not saying that one or two haven't worked, but this takes times." Regina sat forward and pushed my medium-sized pestle toward me with its hefty mortar. "You're going to think about Heidi as you add each ingredient to the spell. We're going to have her call you at the exact moment the clock strikes ten o'clock."

I didn't remind Mom that I'd already been through the basics with Leo. We did this routine almost nightly, with the exception of those evenings when I was too tired to listen to him yammer on about how my pinches were too large.

Those were also the nights I chose to drink wine instead.

"Fine," I murmured, reaching over and turning the spell book toward me. The pages were worn with time, indicating that this magical tome had been around longer than my grandmother. I was still researching my lineage, but Leo's lessons kept me rather busy. "High John the Conqueror Root 1, cinnamon, bay leaves, and Kava Kava."

I immediately reached for the first ingredient, but my mother smacked my hand.

"Ow!" I promptly drew back my arm, rubbing the sting out of my skin. "What was that for?"

"You didn't even stop long enough to think about Heidi or use your energy. Connect with the earth, Raven. Become one with the power you wish to commune with."

Shouldn't this witch stuff be easy? I mean, it's in my blood. Magic was part of my heritage. One would think this kind of thing should come naturally.

It would if you would just open your mind and accept who you really are.

"Breathe in, Raven," my mother said softly, in an almost hypnotic tone. I sat back on my knees and did as she asked, even closing my eyes to take in the scents around me. Cinnamon was one of the first fragrances I recognized, along with my mother's perfume. I pushed away the latter smell to focus on the bay leaves. Something strange began to happen. "That's it, Raven. Let your hand guide you."

I could somewhat sense my mother's touch on my wrist as she steered my hand toward the first bowl. My fingers actually began to tingle. With each ingredient I chose, there was no longer an insecurity about the amount.

It felt right.

"Open your eyes, Raven. Complete the spell."

It was as if I was in my own little world. I was looking through a cast of golden light as I added each ingredient, chanting a spell that would cause Heidi to think of me…reach out to me…need to speak with me. I closed my fingers around the mortar and began to crush the herbs together to bind the spell and the components into one.

I felt one with…

The phone rang.

The golden haze slowly dissipated with what I could only describe as a fading crackling noise, revealing both my mother and Leo smiling.

Yes, Leo was baring his sharp teeth and squinting his eyes in approval. It wasn't that I hadn't been successful in casting other spells, but this…well, this had been different.

Everyone could sense the power in the room.

Those previous incantations had been for health.

This spell had been pure magic—an actual enchantment.

My mother quietly picked up my cell phone that had been on the edge of the coffee table and handed it to me without a word. I could sense her pleasure toward my success, but her green eyes were wary of what she'd just helped accomplish.

"Hello?" I held my breath, even knowing full well that Heidi was on the other end of the line. Her name had been on the display, but I wouldn't be one hundred percent sure the spell was successful until I heard the sound of her voice. "Heidi?"

"Hey, I just got the weirdest vibe that I needed to talk to you. Is everything okay?"

Chapter Nine

"**I** CAN'T BELIEVE my mother actually drove all the way back to the city this morning."

I flipped over the closed sign on the glass door of the tea shop with a little more force than necessary. I was beyond frustrated that my mother was so eager to leave after last night, disappearing as if nothing of substance had taken place.

It had.

I'd created magic.

Enchantments caused people and things to perform a desired action. It's not a simple sphere of magic to cast, because nearly every type of spell required verbal, semantic, and material components.

And I'd succeeded.

I had stayed on the phone with Heidi for around five minutes after receiving her call, assuring her that everything was fine and that I was thinking of her too, which probably explained why she'd felt the need to connect.

We agreed I would see her Friday night when she came to visit.

It wasn't right that I couldn't tell her what was really happening in my life. That's what best friends are for, and yet I was prohibited from revealing the most important part of who I was at the moment.

It figures your mother left. Why stay for the good stuff? She always did tend to run off when this life became too much for her to deal with.

"I don't understand why. I mean, I've never felt connected like that, Leo." I wandered over to the cash register, my knee-high boots still walking on air. Not literally, of course. But I haven't been the same since casting that spell. Honestly, I wanted to recapture that euphoria again and again. "It was like…"

Magic?

"Don't be so trite about such a special milestone," I admonished, shooting him an irate glance. He was gazing out the display window and watching the street lamps come on one by one. The other shops were closing down for the evening, though everyone seemed to have their Christmas lights on a timer to shutdown much later than closing. Within minutes, colorful strands of blinking bulbs lined both sides of River Bay. Seeing as Heidi didn't arrive until tomorrow, I could take the rest of the night to perfect another enchantment. "Let's head back to the house, Leo. I want to try and cast another spell from Nan's magical compendium. Maybe this one can give us some answers about Ben Stanway's murder."

The entire day had been spent hearing about the latest developments on the case from various customers. Candy had been one of the first shoppers of the day, giving her two cents about the rumor of Alison and Oliver Bend committing the murder together wearing rain slickers. That would explain why they didn't get any blood on their clothes.

Candy hadn't specified where she'd heard that piece of gossip, but she was unwavering in her belief of their innocence. I figured someone had been to the salon who was in full support of the Bends.

Otis had come by the shop, too, which was unusual for a Thursday. He usually picked up his special tea blend on Fridays, but he mentioned having a meeting with Detective Swanson tomorrow. Of course, that prompted me to ask the former sheriff what his thoughts were on Ben Stanway's murder.

I couldn't help myself.

Of course, you couldn't.

I didn't bother replying to Leo as I grabbed my purse from underneath the cash register.

You see, Otis caught me unaware when he had suddenly become tightlipped. It was as if we hadn't even been discussing the murder of his fishing buddy. Instead, he'd pulled out his wallet, handed me a twenty-dollar bill, and left the shop in under thirty seconds without another word.

I'm thinking you should charge a bit more.

"I think Otis believes that Oliver Bend is capable of murder," I shared, heading toward the back to grab my coat. I parted the ivory-colored beads that separated the storage room from the main area of the tea shop, reaching in and grabbing my coat off the rack just inside the doorframe. "Doesn't that tell you something?"

Yes. It tells me that Oliver Bend could have killed someone and that we shouldn't be messing around with someone of that ilk—you know, someone capable of that kind of evil.

"Someone of that ilk? Really?"

Sometimes Leo had the strangest vocabulary. I set my purse down on one of the display tables as I put on my jacket and adjusted my scarf. The meteorologist was still talking about a rather large snowstorm headed this way. If the temperature was anything to go by, he was absolutely spot on.

When Leo didn't have a snarky comeback to my question, I glanced up to see if he'd disappeared on me again. It wouldn't have been all that of an unusual occurrence.

Nope, Leo was still in the display window.

Unfortunately, he was now standing on all four paws with his back arched.

Oh, this wasn't a good omen.

"Leo?" I wasn't sure why I'd whispered his name, but it was rather unnerving not to be able to make out what was causing him to be so alarmed. "What is it?"

The knock that came at the front door was more like a bang. I'm pretty sure my feet came off the ground, but I managed to not knock the china off the table next to me.

Lo and behold, one of the auditors was staring back at me through the glass door.

Don't answer it.

With David Laken watching my every move, I didn't want to get caught talking to my cat. It was bad enough that people thought Nan had been a bit of a cuckoo. I certainly didn't need that label attached to me at the age of thirty, talking to my pet as if we were holding a conversation.

I pasted a smile on my face and motioned for the auditor to come on in, seeing as I hadn't flipped the deadbolt.

Do you ever listen to me?

The palm of my hand began to warm the moment Mr. Laken entered the shop. My cell phone was in my purse, but it wasn't like the other shop owners couldn't see inside the store now that it was dark outside. Besides, the police station was right across the street, and Eileen hadn't left for the evening quite yet.

"Mr. Laken, right? We never did get to formally meet," I said with a small smile, stepping forward so that I wasn't so close to the back room. It was hard to stop the visions of him forcing me in the back and knocking me over the head with a teapot. "I'm so sorry about Mr. Stanway's passing. I hope the police find out who did such a horrible thing soon, and that you and your team can get some measure of closure."

Did it ever occur to you that this man is the one responsible?

I wanted to snap at Leo that maybe we'd already have that information if only I'd been able to do more spells last night, but I maintained my gaze on David Laken.

I didn't want to give anything away.

Mr. Laken's cheeks were rather ruddy from the cold weather, and I wondered if he'd walked here from the inn. I didn't recall seeing headlights to indicate a vehicle had parked in front of the shop, but that didn't mean he hadn't found a spot near Mindy's boutique or that I just missed him pulling in.

"I appreciate that, Miss Marigold." It didn't seem that I was such a stranger to him, after all. "It's been a tough few days."

Mr. Laken was a bit overweight, and his dress coat didn't cover up the collar of his shirt that seemed just a bit too tight around his neck. I had to keep my focus on his black rimmed glasses or else I found it hard to swallow.

"I was hoping you could help me with a gift."

"A gift?" I had been under the assumption that he and the rest of his team were driving back to the city for Ben Stanway's funeral. "You mean for Mrs. Stanway? That's a very nice gesture."

"Actually, it's for Ms. Duggan," David Laken said, his cheeks remaining a bit red as he cleared his throat in discomfort. "It's her birthday tomorrow, and I was hoping something from your shop might cheer her up."

Things are about to get interesting.

At first, I thought Leo was referring to the fact that David Laken wanted to get Rachel a gift. I stood corrected when the glass door opened once more, letting a gust of cold air enter...along with Liam.

"Liam, what can I help you with?"

"Actually, I was heading over to the inn to speak with Mr. Laken when I saw him in your shop." Liam never took his eyes off the auditor, whose cheeks somehow became even rosier. "Do you have a few moments to answer a few questions, Mr. Laken?"

"Of course," David replied, somehow fitting a finger inside his collar in an attempt to loosen the fabric. He wasn't going to have much luck, not with that button stretched to the max. "Although I'm not sure how much more I can help. I answered all of Detective Swanson's questions the other day."

"Detective Swanson had some follow up questions that he passed onto me." Liam pointed over to the station with his brown leather gloves that matched his jacket. "Why don't you drop by after you're done with your business here?"

"Oh, please don't feel like you have to head out into the cold." I gestured toward some unique tea flavors, as well as a tea cup that had a cute expression hand-painted on the side. "I have just the thing that Ms. Duggan might like, and I can wrap it up for you in the back to give the two of you some privacy."

"Raven, I don't think that'll be—"

"That works for me," David replied quickly, obviously feeling much more at ease now that he didn't have to step foot into a police station. He set his briefcase on the ground and crossed his arms with a nod. "Please, Sheriff. Ask your questions."

You did that on purpose.

I quietly made my way to the back room before answering Leo.

"Of course, I did," I whispered, removing my dress coat and hanging it up on the coat rack. As quickly as possible, I located the two boxes that would provide me with the gifts I'd promised for Rachel Duggan. "How else are we going to hear what David Laken has to say about the murder?"

We aren't. The last I checked, it wasn't you wearing that pointy badge, driving an SUV with a cage for a back seat, or wearing a six shooter like it's high noon.

"But I told you that we should help." I distinctly remember Neal Edlyn saying that Rachel Duggan preferred tea bags over loose tea leaves. It didn't take me long to choose a dozen assorted flavors out of one of the boxes I'd stored in the back. "Leo, don't you get it? This is how I can use my magic to benefit the community."

You already use your magic to help others. It's true that there have been a few mishaps along the way, but you still help the residents of Paramour Bay with their quality of life.

"I want to do more than that," I replied, keeping my voice as low as possible so that it didn't carry into the main area of the shop. "Now be quiet so that I can hear what they're saying."

I leaned over the corner of the counter that I used when choosing display items, all but pressing my ear to the ivory-colored fairies. It was hard to do so without moving the numerous strings, but I'd found just the right spot to take advantage of the conversation out front.

"...proven that Mr. Edlyn wasn't taking bribes from Oliver Bend," Liam stated, his rich voice easily distinguishable. "Can you think of any other reason that someone would want Mr. Stanway dead?"

"Like I told Detective Swanson, Neal admitted to having a heated argument with Ben the night before he died. That's all I know."

"You mentioned to Detective Swanson that you didn't much care for Mr. Stanway yourself. Did you—"

"Now hold up one second," David replied in a bit of panic. I could just envision him trying to loosen his collar again. "If I remember correctly, I said that Ben wasn't the easiest man to work for. That doesn't mean I killed him. I just meant he could be difficult to work with."

"Was there a specific reason you didn't care for Mr. Stanway's management style?"

"It wasn't his management style I had an issue with. I didn't care for the fact that Ben didn't treat others with respect, ogled the women in our office like it was his own personal harem, and thought his title was better than ours. It wasn't professional. It was downright rude, to tell you the truth. And Neal is no better, for that matter."

Ogle women? Neal didn't strike me as the type of man to ogle any woman. He had asked me out to dinner, but he'd done so in a very respectful manner and had taken my denial like a gentleman.

Had Ben made a pass at Rachel even though he was married? Had Neal?

"I think Mr. Laken is talking about Rachel Duggan," I murmured, almost falling off the corner of the counter when Leo decided to bat at one of the tea bags. "What are you doing?"

Stopping you from making a fool of yourself. Plus...it has a string!

Leo used a paw to swipe at another tea bag, all but forcing me to turn my attention to the gift I was supposed to be wrapping.

You realize that this makes you no better than those two gos-

sips—Elsie and Wilma.

"But I'm trying to help solve Ben Stanway's murder," I protested, although it didn't sound as convincing as it should have. Maybe Leo had a point. I'd been successful on a half-dozen spells, and only one that didn't have to do with illnesses of some sort. I had allowed myself to get caught up in the investigation, when I really had no right to put my nose somewhere that it didn't belong. "Fine. I'll gift wrap these items for David Laken, and then we can head home—on one condition."

The answer is no. Heidi can't know that you're a witch.

"That wasn't the condition I was going to offer up, but since we're on the topic—"

"Raven? Who are you talking to?"

I'd been so busy wrapping up Mr. Laken's gift to Ms. Duggan that I hadn't been paying attention to the front of the shop. Liam had spoken before he'd parted the strings, causing a chaos of clicking noises. There was no way out of answering his question, so I swallowed my pride and became a younger version of an old cat lady.

"Leo," I exclaimed, giving Liam a little shrug while smiling in chagrin. "You know how cats can be. He was knocking things to the floor and making my job harder than necessary."

Why do you always blame me?

"I appreciate the privacy you offered us. I'll let you conclude your business with Mr. Laken." Liam's gaze was drawn to the floor, not that I could blame him. It's where Heidi and I had discovered a dead body…apparently, the first one of many since I'd arrived in town. I was hoping that Ben Stanway was the last. "Did I hear you say that Mr. Laken is buying something for Rachel Duggan?"

"Yes, you heard me correctly." I carefully put the finishing touches on the ribbon. A stab of guilt had gone through me at Liam's gratitude for something I hadn't given him. Oh, this wasn't good. I was going to have to come clean. "There's something I need to tell you."

Don't do it.

"You see…"

I thought you wanted that date? This is a surefire way to make sure that never happens. Maybe that's for the best, though.

"I offered you the shop to speak with Mr. Laken so that I could overhear his answers." My words had practically been rushed together, but then again, I had never been a good liar. It was probably why I was having such a hard time keeping this witchcraft stuff from Heidi. It didn't feel right. "I'm sorry. That was wrong of me, and it won't happen again."

You just had to spill the beans, didn't you?

"Raven, I knew all along you were listening to every word," Liam said with a charming smile, keeping his voice low enough so that Mr. Laken didn't get wind of my confession. "I don't blame you, especially given that you were there at the time of the murder. It's only natural for you to be curious as to who the police are looking at as suspects."

Is this guy for real?

Leo began to hack up what sounded like a hairball, but I was certain that he was feigning a gag reflex to the sweet intentions of this conversation.

"I'm still going over that day, thinking maybe I saw something that could help you."

Are you literally paving the way to use a spell?

"It would definitely help the investigation if you could remember something that stood out."

"It's why I mentioned Mr. Laken buying a gift for Ms. Duggan when you came in. I thought it was odd, given that the two are just co-workers, even if it is her birthday."

Did you know that your good ol' sheriff bought Eileen a Christmas present? I overheard him talking to Mindy the other day. So basically, you just told him that it was wrong of him to buy his own dispatcher a gift.

I refrained from pushing Leo off the counter…just barely.

Liam nodded, though he didn't technically agree with me.

See? You might have just blown your chance.

"You could be onto something there," Liam finally said, glancing over his shoulder at presumably the man we were speaking about. "I should head back to the station and give Jack a call. I'll touch base with you about dinner after Heidi heads back to the city. Is that okay?"

"That sounds fantastic." I managed to act like an adult woman rather than my usual excited crazy self where I had to bite my lip to keep myself from screaming aloud. "Enjoy your weekend."

I was a day early in that blessing, considering today was only Thursday. It didn't matter, though. Liam understood what I meant as he left the fairy beads to create chaotic music after his departure.

Are you sure you're thirty years old and not ten?

"I'm old enough to know when someone's being a third wheel." I arched my eyebrow at the same time I picked up the beautifully giftwrapped tea bags and cup that I'd put together, proud of my abilities to tie a bow. "Now it's time to head home and work on a spell, so sashay your butt on to the house. I'll meet you there."

Remember, Leo appeared and disappeared at will. I still wasn't sure how he managed to get back and forth between the house and the shop, but I'm sure the ability came with others I wasn't even aware Leo kept underneath that matted fur.

"Mr. Laken, I do believe I have the perfect gift for you to give to Ms. Duggan," I called out after leaving the backroom. "It's all gift wrapped, and I made sure to remove the price tags."

"Please, call me David." His ruddy cheeks were finally fading back to his original color. Liam's questions must not have affected him too much. "That is perfect. I know how much Rachel loves her tea."

"Your colleague, Neal Edlyn, stopped by yesterday. I didn't realize you were working with so many tea lovers," I said, initiating conversation while I rang up his purchase.

"Neal has his own way of doing things. He's a bit of a tea snob," David replied, lifting one half of his lip in what seemed like contempt. The palm of my hand began to tingle. "Everything has to be picture perfect. We're talking even the staples have to be seamlessly horizontal against the paper. Let's just say the last few days have been an adjustment since Ben's death."

What is it about you that people feel the need to share every detail of their life?

"Are you taking the day off tomorrow with your team to attend Mr. Stanway's funeral?" I managed not to frown when David handed me a fifty-dollar bill instead of using a credit card. "I truly am sorry for your loss."

David appeared as if he wanted to say something in response to my offered condolences, but he remained quiet as he took the change I'd gathered from the cash register. He stood there a bit longer than I thought appropriate without responding.

Is he having a heart attack? He keeps staring at his wallet as if he's going to keel over any second.

I wish Leo had taken my advice and headed back home. Instead, he was here to witness whatever was about to happen…and it was a doozy.

"Ms. Marigold, I heard what your grandmother did for Ben. Do you think you could provide me with a protection spell, as well?"

Chapter Ten

*A*BSOLUTELY NOT.

"I don't understand why this is such a big deal," I argued, having already handed Ted a list of items I'd need for the protection spell. I'd also included the special ingredients for the vision incantation that I'd like to try in summoning the last moments Ben Stanway experienced right before he was murdered. "David Laken is a paying customer whom was already aware of the services provided by the shop. It's not like I'm going to turn him away."

I had all but pleaded with David to go to Liam about his fears of being the killer's next target. The auditor wouldn't dream of it, saying that the police would think he'd gone crazy. Nothing I said or did had changed his mind, and I'm pretty sure the only reason he left the shop was because I'd given him my word I would work on a protection blend.

You aren't strong enough to create a protection spell, and don't think I didn't see that additional list you handed off to Ted. You're going to blow us to Kingdom Come. Spell failure can have devastating consequences.

"You saw what I did last night when Mom was here." Reminding Leo of my success was the only way I was going to succeed in casting the spell I'd all but promised a scared man. "You also saw how frightened David was when he requested my help. I know he didn't say it, but I think he believes Neal Edlyn *did* in fact kill Ben Stanway. If I can prove it, then Liam can make the arrest."

Stop. Just stop. You're getting too big for your britches.

I'd walked around the coffee table where I'd set out the various pestles and mortars I'd need for the upcoming lesson. It technically wasn't a lesson, but rather an actual walkthrough of two major incantations that I was determined to make happen tonight. I didn't have time to stop and contemplate, but I also knew I needed Leo's guidance.

Why won't you listen to reason, Raven?

It was the first time since I'd known Leo that he actually asked me a serious question. I made myself comfortable on the fluffy pillow and grabbed my wine for a bit of courage. This would either make or break our bond, and I really needed him by my side if I was going to be successful at practicing witchcraft.

Otherwise, I might as well pack up and return to the city.

"Everything I said the other day was true," I confessed about my reasons for wanting to find Ben Stanway's murderer. It was weird speaking to Leo about this. I mean, not really. We chatted about it all the time. I'm referring to the serious undertone of this conversation. "Mom all but ignored our lineage, Leo. She kept my identity and my abilities from me for close to thirty years. That wasn't fair to anyone involved, and I still have residual anger over the fact that there was a rift between us and Nan."

Go on.

Leo was really making it hard to continue when he made me feel as if I were lying on the couch in some stuffy psychiatrist's office.

"I've already explained this to you, but helping out the town by finding out whoever murdered Ben Stanway can be part of my contribution. It's important to me to know that I've done my part to make this a safe community."

Oh, I get it. You have a sense of guilt over Flo Akers. It's understandable.

"Would you stop patronizing me?" I all but demanded in irritation. A sip of wine did nothing to give me more patience. "Yes, I have remorse over what Flo did to Jacob Blackleach."

Do you want to stop here and catch the reader up on exactly what we're talking about? They're probably confused.

"Fine," I grumbled, not really wanting to remind myself about the day I'd arrived in Paramour Bay. I took another healthy sip of wine to get me through the story I was about to tell you. "But don't think this gets you out of helping me tonight, Leo."

You see, dear reader, Flo Akers had been a waitress over at Trixie's Diner. She had been part of the community, and everyone loved her. Well, almost everyone. She had red hair, chewed gum, and was one of the first to welcome me to this town. I thought she was a sweet, sweet woman.

I was wrong.

Boy, were you ever wrong.

"Leo, this is my story to tell."

Let's continue or else we'll never get to this evening's objective, which is the casting of spells.

Flo was friends with Cora Barnes. You remember, the woman who has a dislike for me because I'm the spawn of Satan, which she truly believes is my mother?

I didn't know it at the time, but Cora was sharing the magical tea blend that contained a youth spell with the ladies' auxiliary club...which Flo happened to be a part of. When Cora and I had a falling out over how rude she was to my family, I cut off her supply to Nan's special brew.

You can imagine how that went over—like a ton of bricks.

Wait.

I need to backtrack for a second.

Flo thought Jacob Blackleach was trying to steal the tea blend and whatever else my Nan had hidden away in the store. So, she hit him over the head with one of the stone pestle bowls I keep in the shop to blend different tea leaves to a consistent texture. What she didn't know was that she did, in fact, do the Marigolds a favor by eliminating a member of the Blackleach coven who wanted access to my Nan's spell book.

Not that I'm condoning murder for any reason.

I'm not.

Not in any way, shape, or form.

So, your guilt over Flo's crazy obsession about aging is why you want to put our lives in danger when you aren't even close to the stage you'd need to be to cast either of these spells. That's just...insane. I mean, you're basically inviting the killer to walk right on in here to take us both out. Not to mention what that kind of power release might attract, including the attention of another coven.

"What do you mean?"

"Certain spells are like mirrors," Ted said, coming through the door with a basketful of herbs, petals, and other ingredients.

I waited for Ted to continue, but as usual he remained silent as he handed over the wicker basket. The pads of my fingers tingled the moment I brushed over a white rose petal. I met Leo's gaze to find he was quietly observing me with his larger green eye. A spark of excitement shot through me.

"It's happening, isn't it? I'm getting stronger. I connected." I set my wine glass down next to one of the pestles and tucked my legs underneath me to give me a bit of height on the pillow. "Leo, this is amazing."

Leo sighed in acceptance, having recognized the progression of my gift. There was no stopping it, and he had no choice but to carefully cultivate my...powers? I wasn't sure what to call them as of yet, but this had to be the most exciting time of my life. It was as if I was coming of age.

We spent the next ten minutes finding a spell that would take my sight back to Monday at the exact time I'd walked through the door of the B&B. It was pointless to cast a protection incantation for David Laken if it turned out that he was in fact the killer. I wasn't sure what I'd see during the vision, but I'd worry about how best to tell Liam the identity of the killer afterward.

You need to concentrate on your memory of walking through the door of the inn, Raven. It's very important that you put yourself in that exact moment when—

I'd been half-listening to Leo as my gaze traveled over the written words on the page, but the way he'd abruptly stopped talking had sure caught my attention.

"Leo?"

I glanced up from the treasured spell book to find Leo standing on his back legs. He reminded me of one of those mongooses I'd seen on television, with his back straight and his head practically on a swivel.

I experienced nothing that told me we were in danger, so I wasn't sure what had caught his attention. Ted didn't appear out of sorts, so maybe his reaction had something to do with his short-term memory loss.

Hide the pestles! Grab the blanket and toss it over the coffee table. Quick!

"Leo, what are you carrying on about now?"

Did you not understand me?

Leo landed on all fours, only to then run around in two quick circles. He stopped and tilted his head as he stared at me, obviously having forgotten what had him so riled up. His short-term memory had clearly gotten the best of him.

That was odd.

Leo sat back down and licked his front right paw as if nothing had happened.

Are you ready to begin?

"Surprise!" We all jumped at the sound of Heidi's voice, though our reaction was most likely due to the heavy wooden door that unexpectedly opened with a bang. "Pour the wine and get ready for a heck of a story! I can't wait to tell you who I saw at the train station. I was just standing there and—"

Heidi stopped talking completely. She stood in the doorway with an overnight bag in one hand, her oversized purse strung over her right shoulder, and her mouth hanging open at the sight of materials in front of me.

I feel sick.

It was probably a hairball, though I couldn't rule out stress from the upcoming confrontation. Heidi was my best friend, and she knew me better than anyone. She always recognized when I lied, when I needed help, and when I needed a shoulder to cry on.

Right now?

I was supposed to lie, but the truth bubbled up in the back of my throat before I could think to stop it.

Nooooo!

Leo's voice was like an echo that continued forever, but his plea wasn't enough to prevent the truth from spilling out of my red painted lips.

"I'm a witch!" I exclaimed, jumping to my feet and stepping off the pillow. A heavy weight was finally lifted off my shoulders. "There. I said it. It's out. I'm a witch, Heidi!"

Chapter Eleven

"TELL ME THAT'S real coffee I smell, and not the stuff I've been spooning out of a jar."

Heidi's words basically came out as one big moan, but I understood what she trying to convey. Her blonde hair looked as if she'd stuck her finger into an electrical socket. Her bloodshot eyes told anyone looking how much wine she'd consumed last night, and she no longer looked upon Leo as a hapless rescue kitty who needed an endless supply of kisses.

I blame you.

It was the first time Leo had spoken to me since I blurted out to Heidi that I was a witch. Such an admission was unacceptable according to those mystical bylaws that I've yet to be afforded an opportunity to read myself.

The thing of it was…I didn't give two hoots.

The relief after such a confession was a massive reprieve from the horrible guilt I had to choke down for excluding my best friend in the entire world.

"It *is* coffee," I replied, having already poured Heidi a full mug of caffeine with a lot of sugar and a hint of cream. "Sit down and drink up. We have to be at the store in twenty minutes."

Heidi sat down on one of the stools at the island, the palm of her hand still resting against her forehead. There was probably some type of spell that could cure a hangover, but I doubted that I could take away the pounding headache without freaking her out. I paused in my thinking—maybe I should give her some proof of the gift my lineage had bestowed upon me.

Heidi finally opened both eyes to stare suspiciously down at the coffee cup.

"Did you..." Heidi pressed her index finger to her nose and wiggled it back and forth.

Why does everyone assume witches are like Elizabeth?

"No, I didn't make the coffee with magic." I didn't want to regret telling Heidi the truth, but she didn't look at me like her best friend anymore. She scrutinized every move I made last night as if I were about to summon up the Devil himself. I'd have to change to her mind. "Heidi, I'm still me."

The way you're going with your lessons, it wouldn't surprise me if some demon popped through the veil and pulled your pigtails.

"What? That can happen?" I asked as panic began to fill my soul. I loved my soul. I didn't want it taken over by some evil doer. "Leo, can demons really—"

"Demons? As in down below? Is there someone else here with us?" Heidi was wide awake now, and maybe even hangover free. She was completely alert as she scanned the kitchen in a slow circle until she'd searched every square inch of the main level. "I've seen those horror movies with the Ouija boards. It never turns out well for the visiting friend from the city. Those boards are portals, Raven. Portals. Maybe your mom is right. You should come back to the city and pretend this place never existed."

It might be time to teach you a revision spell. This situation never needs to be remembered, and things can go back to normal.

"Heidi, I'm disappointed in you." It was easier to ignore Leo than it was to reply to such a ludicrous suggestion. I wasn't going to take away Heidi's memories. That was as bad as stealing. "I'm still me. Leo just made a wisecrack, and I fell for it for just a second. He also asked why everyone thought witches were like the actress from the television show. The way he said it made me believe he knew Elizabeth Montgomery personally. That's all."

I did know her, and she was a beautiful, intelligent woman. That doesn't mean I don't blame her for starting the nose twitching thing. Such silliness. She's probably still laughing on the other side while having tea with Rosemary.

"Raven, I've always considered myself a fairly rational person." Heidi had placed both of her hands over her chest, as if she were pleading with me to understand what she was going through. "Now you're spouting all this nonsense about witches, talking cats, and magical spells. There's only so much a girl can take on faith."

That's why I'm opting for a revision spell.

"We're not doing that," I said through clenched teeth, realizing I'd only made things worse with Heidi when she locked her gaze on Leo as if he'd grown horns. "Heidi, Leo was just suggesting—"

You might not want to tell her we can erase her memory.

That was actually the first good advice Leo had given me all morning.

"What was Leo suggesting?" Heidi continued to stare at Leo with caution as she tightened the lapels on her pink and yellow robe. "Tell me."

"Leo's concerned about the man who was murdered on Monday at the B&B." I had to come up with something, and maybe this would garner her interest. "You see, we were going to cast a spell that could help with the investigation."

Tell her the truth, Raven. I said that we should stay far away from…

Leo continued to rant while I studied Heidi carefully. She remained quiet as she cautiously reached for the coffee mug she'd left on the counter. She'd definitely had too much wine while I told her about my newfound gift well into the wee hours of the night. Nothing was going to cure her hangover, but I might be able to sway her opinion on the witchcraft angle while she was still shaking out the cobwebs.

"You remember those old murder movies we used to watch?" I was trying to get Heidi to think back to when we would binge watch Lifetime movies and try to figure out who the bad guy was while we ate way too much popcorn and drank hot chocolate. "We were good at it, but imagine if I could use a spell to help Liam to find a clue so that he can make an arrest. Better yet, what do you think Detective Swanson would do if you were to give your opinion on how it went down…and you led him to the murderer by sharing your perspective!"

You want to die, don't you?

"I do not," I protested, wincing when I wasn't able to stop myself from replying to Leo. The familiar look of panic was crossing Heidi's face again, and I began to wonder if she thought I was certifiably insane. "You told me last night that you ran into Detective Swanson and that you were interested in having dinner with him."

"Jack would carry me away in a straitjacket if I told him you were a witch that casts magic spells." Heidi finally took a drink of her coffee. Hopefully, the caffeine would kick in soon. She looked me straight in the eye, and I could see the clarity forming in her mind. "Do a spell for me."

"Do a…"

What? No. That's a bad idea.

"Why? It would prove to her that I am what I say I am."

Tell her to put her coffee cup down.

"Why?"

Tell her before I change my mind.

"Fine." I crossed my arms and did as Leo instructed. "Put your coffee cup down, Heidi."

I had an inkling about what Leo was about to do, and he was right in protecting my hardwood floors. Heidi would no doubt drop the cup and smash it into bits and pieces once she witnessed Leo in action.

"Why?" Heidi repeated my question, but she slowly leaned forward until she set the cup down on the granite countertop of the island. "Are you going to—"

The scream that Heidi elicited at the sight of Leo disappearing into thin air wasn't unexpected, but the shriek did kind of hurt my eardrums.

I should have covered my ears.

"Did you see that?" Heidi asked frantically, spinning in another circle until she was facing me once more. "Where did Leo go? Is it a mirage or did he really just...poof?"

"He poofed." It wasn't the description I would have used to define Leo's tendency to vanish into thin air, but it was good enough to explain his gift. "But if you need me to cast a spell, I will. I'll admit I'm still learning and that I might have caught my blouse on fire last week by mistake, but you have to understand that it's not easy being a novice witch."

"Tell Leo to come back," Heidi demanded, her eyes searching every nook and cranny of the kitchen. Leo had jumped onto the island before he disappeared, but that didn't stop Heidi from searching the rest of the house. "Can he hear you even when he's not here?"

"Unfortunately, yes," I replied wryly, not surprised when Leo suddenly appeared on the stool that Heidi had vacated a few minutes prior. "And there he is with his pleasant attitude."

My attitude is fine, thank you. Yours, on the other hand, needs an adjustment.

"Heidi, please go get dressed." I glanced at the clock. We were running out of time, and we needed to get to the shop so I could get things ready for the day. What I really wanted was to work on a couple of spells, and I also had to figure out how to tell David Laken that his protection spell wouldn't be ready until Monday at the very earliest. That should be perfect, considering that the auditors had probably left town this morning for Ben Stanway's funeral. "I promise you that we'll talk about this some more, but I have to open the store."

Heidi was wagging her finger in the air, her blue eyes suddenly brightening from her previous cloud of uncertainty.

Oh, I've seen that look before.

It wasn't good.

The last time my best friend had that glimmer in her eyes, I almost ended up in jail for nefarious reasons I won't mention here.

Why couldn't she have been a Marigold?

"What does that mean?" I asked, ignoring Heidi's tilted head as she tried to figure out the conversation.

Look at her.

Leo sighed, almost in the same manner as I did when staring at Liam when he left the police station for lunch.

She would have made the most wonderful witch.

"Did your short-term memory problem kick in?"

No, but you're the one who let the cat out of the bag. It's some-

thing I must accept.

Leo totally meant that pun, but it wasn't worth quibbling about. As he'd said earlier, the damage was done. I wasn't going to do a revision spell, and the relief that my best friend could now be told the details of my life was palpable.

"Do you know what we could do with your...gift?" Heidi grabbed her coffee again, making me believe that I shouldn't have made it extra strong. And my relief was dwindling by the second. "We could win the lottery."

Was she smoking my catnip?

"Heidi, it doesn't work like—"

"Take the day off, Raven," Heidi pleaded, missing the fact that Leo looked ready to hurl up a hairball. "Let's cast a spell that will have us buying the winning lottery ticket. Do you know how many of our problems that would solve in an instant?"

"Listen to me," I said, purposefully walking around the island to stand in front of Heidi so that she couldn't misinterpret what I was going to say. I even took ahold of both her shoulders so that I had her undivided attention. "My gift isn't to be used to enrich myself with worldly goods, Heidi. It's to be cherished. It is to help others, and I need to honor that legacy. What you're talking about is black magic, and that comes with a very hefty price which you can't pay with money."

Tell me about it.

"But you have the ability to..." Heidi allowed her voice to trail off in disappointment. She even looked ready to cry, but that could have easily been from her hangover.

"I'll show you."

What will you show her? I've already shown her everything she needs to see.

It was evident that Leo's concern had risen exponentially, but

I could finally prove to Heidi that my gift should be used very carefully. I quickly walked over to the coffee table, seeing what ingredients I had on hand that I hadn't used last night. There were some items in my kitchen that could be thrown into the mix.

It wasn't long until I had everything needed to make the hangover cure of the century.

You surprise me once in a while, but this was a good idea. Do you mind adding in a few ingredients to—

"No, Leo. I'm not taking away her memories."

I wiggled into the fluffy pillow, glad I'd yet to put on my knee-high boots. Heidi had remained standing near the island, her coffee most likely cold as ice by now. I would have thought I'd be self-conscious having someone watch me work, but Heidi was my best friend. There was nothing I couldn't do in front of her, and this would prevent her from having any more doubts about my gift.

I'm going on record that I don't agree with this.

"Please do the spell with me."

Fine.

Leo took his seat on the couch facing me, curling his bent tail around himself the best he could.

Concentrate on health. Focus on vitality.

Leo continued to guide me, just as my Nan would have wanted. I opened myself up like I did when my mother was here, and it wasn't long before everything began to fade into the background. My sole focus was the concentrated energy within myself.

I began to recite the magical words needed to bring Heidi good health.

My world became smaller, as if Mother Nature was wrapping

her arms around me in a warm shield that protected and soothed my soul. This intimate sensation was how I understood that I was using my powers for good.

Curse words expressing disbelief oddly came to mind, but they weren't falling from my lips. They were actually being verbalized by Heidi, who had witnessed everything in those enchanted moments.

"D-did you see that? Those petals," Heidi exclaimed, pointing at my workstation in front of me. "Those white ones were floating in the air. Did you do that?"

Very good, Raven. You're getting better at this. I'm thinking another spell is in order to prevent Heidi from telling anyone. You know, some sort of incantation that silences the storyteller. Or we could just sew her lips together. Yep. That would be much easier.

Excitement blossomed throughout my chest until I wanted to scream with joy, but I realized that we were really late in opening the tea shop. Responsibilities were never far away. I scrambled to my feet, stepping off the large pillow and racing into the kitchen. I shooed Heidi away, ordering her to take a quick shower and dress. By the time she'd returned, I had a steaming cup of hot tea waiting for her on the counter.

"Drink," I ordered her, leaning my abdomen against the island so I could watch the effects of the tea up close. "All of it."

Heidi lifted one of her perfectly manicured eyebrows as she stared at the cup of tea in front of her.

I edged it closer.

She's not a bug underneath a microscope.

"Heidi, drink the tea."

"Fine," she replied with a sigh of resignation.

She lifted the small porcelain cup to her lips and began to consume the concoction. By the time she was finished, the pale tint to her flesh had been erased and replaced with a healthy tone.

Right in front of me, the bloodshot tint to her eyes faded until her blue eyes were sparkling with the same excitement as when she'd witnessed the floating rose petals.

"It worked. Raven, this is absolutely amazeballs."

And just like that, I was confident that we could solve Ben Stanway's murder.

Chapter Twelve

*Y*OU'RE GOING TO *send me to an early grave.*

"I thought Nan fixed that when she kept you alive the first time around."

I continued to stare out the display window until the street posts began to light up one by one. The reds, blues, and greens of the holiday lights were now more vivid, and the flurries that had been drifting down from the darkening sky were getting larger and faster with every passing second.

The storm had finally arrived, and it looked to be a doozy.

It's a good thing Ted got us supplies. I was running out of cat-nip, anyway.

"Where is she?"

The *she* who I was referring to was Heidi.

She'd bundled up in her ski jacket, scarf, hat, and gloves around two hours ago with the purpose of visiting the wax museum. I'd done my best to tell her that was not a good idea, but she'd gotten it into her head that Oliver and Alison Bend were the ones responsible for Ben Stanway's murder.

Now you know how I feel.

"Leo, that's different. By using a spell to help solve the investigation, I'm not putting myself in any immediate danger." How long did it take to look at wax statues anyway? A quick glance at my cell phone revealed that it was almost five o'clock. I would just have to go searching for Heidi myself the second I flipped over the closed sign. "I don't know why you didn't go with her."

It's just not the same.

Leo had been lamenting over the fact that Heidi now treated him differently than before. She used to pick him up, love on him, give him special treats, and basically indulge his every whim.

She now looks at me as if I have horns. This is all your fault, you know. You've stolen my free ride on the love train.

"It's not my fault that she walked into the house unexpectedly. And would you stop looking like you lost your best friend?"

I'm allowed to grieve. Besides, you need to change things back to the way they were. We've upset the balance of things, and that is never a good…

Leo let his words trail off, and once again I got the feeling that he wasn't telling me something.

"Leo, I asked this before, but does something bad happen if someone outside of our world knows our secret?"

Two things happened to prevent Leo from answering me—Leo hissed at the front door and the palm of my hand immediately became warm.

"Brrr," a man said after having entered the shop. The bell above door was still ringing back and forth by the time I identified the customer. "It's freezing out there."

"David, what are you doing here?" I tried my best to stop my heart from beating out of my chest. I didn't have his protection spell, but he wasn't even supposed to be in town. He and the other auditors should all be back in the city for Ben Stanway's funeral. "Why are you still in Paramour Bay?"

"Didn't you hear? We ended up working all day today instead of driving back to the city. The storm that's now overhead closed down some of the major highways. It wasn't in our best interest to leave town." David didn't even take notice of Leo standing on all four paws with his back arched. His larger green eye was practically glued to me. "Do you have it?"

"I'm sorry, but I thought you were out of town until Monday. Your special tea blend is not ready." I could literally see the panic settle in the man's eyes at the thought of returning to the inn without the protection spell. "David, who is it that you're afraid of? Neal? We can easily go to the sheriff and tell him that you—"

"No!" David practically shouted, reaching out to steady himself by using one of the display tables. I waited for the white tablecloth to slide off, causing the rest of the items on the table to fall to the floor. All was safe when he steadied the fabric with his hand. "I'm sorry. I didn't mean to yell. I would just feel safer having the protection spell, seeing as my entire team has to stay in town this weekend."

Is this guy for real? I've seen better acting on daytime TV.

Leo was right, in a way.

David was being rather dramatic, but I could use that to my advantage.

"David, it would help to know if it's a male or a female you need protection from." I cautiously walked out from behind the register, believing he would be more upfront with me if he saw my desire to help him. "It's not like I'm a witch who can cast spells. I only whip up tea blends that heightens your awareness to your surroundings."

After David had asked me to create a protection spell for him, I had to explain what my Nan had done for Ben Stanway in a way that didn't make it sound as if she'd used real magic. David hadn't seemed convinced, especially given that Ben had run out of tea shortly after my grandmother had passed away. That alone had influenced David's thoughts in needing his own protection spell.

"It's…" David couldn't get his declaration out. He pulled out his wallet and some cash—more than what I would charge for a typical spell—and held the money out to me. "I'll pay you whatever you want. I just need protection."

Does this guy really believe that money can buy him anything?

"Ben obviously confided in you," I pointed out, trying to ease David's concern while attempting to understand the situation. Answers were just questions away. "Please tell me who Ben was afraid of so that we can go to the police."

"If I tell you, will you promise to make me that tea? I'm not ready to die."

I'm going to need popcorn and a soda for this.

"Yes," I promised, fully intending to follow through. "Who was Ben afraid of?"

"That's the problem," David whispered anxiously, leaning closer to attempt once more to give me his money. I stepped back. "Ben didn't know who was trying to kill him."

Sounds like Ben Stanway might have just cracked under the stress of his job. You know, it happens all the time to nonbelievers.

"Why would Ben believe someone was trying to kill him to begin with?" I asked, finally getting somewhere. Technically, David's performance these last few days ruled him out as a suspect. "What was his reasoning to come to my grandmother for a protection spell? And did you ever tell the police about his needing protection?"

Why would you rule him out as a suspect? Those cozy mystery writers always try to throw you off, so don't for one second believe that David Laken couldn't be the guilty party. He probably did something wrong.

David's cheeks were still ruddy, and I doubted it had anything to do with the bitter temperature outside. It was almost as if he were trying not to break down and cry.

"The police?" David shook his head in disappointment. I had apparently lost status in his opinion for asking such a question. "What could we say that didn't make Ben sound like he was a paranoid lunatic? Can you imagine any of us telling Detective Swanson that Ben bought a protection spell? He didn't even tell his old fishing buddy about it."

"Otis didn't know that Ben came to my grandmother asking for help?"

"No. Ben was a very proud man," David explained, still holding the cash in his hand with a tight grip. "The only reason the team knew the drastic steps he'd taken was because he'd become obsessed with that tea he was drinking every day."

"I don't understand."

Join the club. We're having a mixer later tonight.

David glanced out the window toward the police station. He thinned his lips together, almost as if he were debating whether or not to take a chance on coming clean with the police.

If he won't, you will.

True.

My next move after David left my shop was to make a beeline for Liam's office. This information could be of use in the investigation, and I hadn't had to use witchcraft to seek out any answers, either.

Could we keep that status quo, then? I'd like to get through this without attracting any attention on our little operation here.

"Rachel had run out of tea in the office one day. Everyone by then had known Ben was drinking the stuff, so she didn't think it would hurt to go into his office and take some." David seemed to have made an internal decision, because he took a step forward and then around me to reach the counter. He set the thick wad of cash next to the credit card machine. "Ben freaked out on Rachel, and then he was left with no choice but to explain why when she threatened to go to human resources after being frightened by his antics."

It all comes full circle.

"Ben didn't tell everyone that he believed someone was out to kill him. He only confided in Rachel," I surmised, hitting the jackpot when David nodded his approval. "David, what did Ben tell her?"

"Ben told Rachel all the little things that had occurred, like the ones happening to me." So, we finally get to the crux of the story. "Ben thought someone was following him. He would receive phone calls in the middle of the day, but no one was on the other end of the line. He'd open his emails and some messages would be marked as read when he hadn't opened them. Someone *was* watching him, and then there was the voicemail."

"What voicemail?"

"The one that said if he didn't do the right thing, he'd die."

Well, that was rather prophetic given the circumstances.

"Did you have a copy of that voicemail?"

"No. I believe Ben erased it." David motioned for me to come around the cash register so that I could take his money. "But I thought I saw someone watching me when I walked into Oliver Bend's office this morning."

"Weren't you with the others all day?"

"No, I slept through my alarm and was running around fifteen minutes late." David gestured toward the money. "I've told you everything. Now will you make me that tea? And a lot of it!"

I think he might crack under the pressure. His cheeks are getting redder by the minute.

"I have a better idea." It was more than apparent that Ben Stanway had been hiding something a lot more interesting than the fact that he'd gone to see a local witch about a spell. "We're going over to the police station right now so that you can tell the sheriff what is going on. Liam can protect you, as well as Detective Swanson."

"They will both think that I'm—"

"They won't think anything other than you're finally telling them the whole truth." I figured I'd cut right to the chase. "David Laken, do you want to die?"

That was a bit harsh, Raven.

"No! That's why I came to you in the first place," David exclaimed, clearly not seeing the simple solution in front of him. Leo was right. His face had become an awful shade of red. "The team and I made a pact *not* to tell the police, because they'll think we're just as crazy as Ben was toward the end."

"Do *you* think that Ben was crazy?"

I left him standing in front of the cash register while I walked to the backroom to retrieve my winter coat. Taking this information to Liam *was* the right thing to do. In all honesty, I couldn't believe that this team of auditors had made a pact over something so vital to the investigation.

Were you at home last night? Do you not remember Heidi's reaction to your declaration of being a witch?

"No, Ben wasn't crazy," David stated emphatically, shoving his wallet into the back pocket of his pants. He'd left the money near the cash register, which reminded me that I still had Neal Edlyn's black leather gloves. "Ben is dead, so he was obviously right in his assumption that someone wanted to kill him. But I cannot break my promise to the team. We'd all likely be fired for not reporting Ben's...well, mental lapse over using something like a protection spell at work."

It didn't take me long to collect my things. It was more than evident to me that someone on David's team killed Ben Stanway. Why else convince everyone to keep silent when they could have easily told the police every detail with the exception of Ben's decision to use witchcraft?

It appeared to me that someone was doing their best to keep everyone quiet, under the guise that not keeping their silence would jeopardize their jobs. That was quite selfish, considering that their boss was dead.

Who was the ringleader?

The obvious choice was Neal Edlyn, right?

Hmmm. You make a good point.

I raised an eyebrow at Leo as I shrugged into my jacket before wrapping my scarf around my neck. Leo was constantly telling me to rely on my senses, so I was going to do just that.

"David, you need to man up. You can't hold out on the investigators."

Ouch.

"Don't worry about what others think of you. You won't be fired, either. Ben Stanway was murdered, and someone you work with doesn't want the police to know that he believed his life was in danger." I slung the straps of my oversized purse over my right shoulder before collecting Neal's gloves. I had a feeling that I would be seeing him shortly, especially considering the auditors were stuck here in Paramour Bay for the weekend. "What does that tell you, David?"

His eyes became rather large as my words finally penetrated

the anxiety he'd worked up over the past ten minutes.

"You believe one of them killed Ben."

"Bingo."

"So I am in danger!"

I wasn't so sure I believed David's life was in jeopardy. Being in any type of situation like the one he'd found himself in could easily cause one's imagination to run wild. It was always better to be safe than sorry, which was why he needed to come clean with the police.

The bell above the door chimed to signal that Heidi had finally made her way back to the shop from her trip to the wax museum, saving me the short trip to find her. Leo had managed to turn away from the door, physically displaying his disappointment with the pretty blonde's reaction to his ability to disappear at will.

Maybe your mother was right. Rosemary cursed me with that dark magic.

There had to be a way to fix things between Leo and Heidi, but it would have to wait.

"Heidi, this is David Laken. He's one of the auditors staying at the inn," I informed my best friend, who was clearly bubbling with excitement. I'd have to find out about her trek through the wax museum later, seeing as we had things to do. "I was just about to escort Mr. Laken over to the police station so that he could tell the sheriff about Ben's belief that someone wanted to kill him."

"You don't have to go anywhere, Mr. Laken," Heidi informed David, her blue eyes shining with eagerness. "I believe an arrest is about to be made in the case. You're not going to believe this, but Detective Swanson just served a search warrant for the wax museum."

Finally! All of this can now be over, and we can get back to your proper lessons. By the way, you wouldn't reconsider using that reverse spell on Heidi, would you? I could use the attention.

Chapter Thirteen

*T*HIS IS A *colossal mistake. I take back everything I said about Heidi making a good witch. You two are going to get the three of us killed in the end, and your grandmother's spell to keep me on this plane of existence will be for naught.*

"Stop with the theatrics, Leo," I muttered, burrowing my face into my scarf as Heidi and I continued to walk down River Bay toward the inn. The snowstorm was in full swing. No one was getting in or out of Paramour Bay. As it was, Heidi and I only had enough time to drop off Neal Edlyn's gloves at the inn before very slowly driving my non-tracked car to my house on the opposite end of town. "We're just making a quick pit stop before we head home for the weekend."

The Christmas lights that had been wrapped around a pine tree in front of the inn blinked steadily through the snowfall. You know the ones I mean—the bulbs about the size of Texas that make your electricity bill skyrocket.

Don't get me wrong. The lights looked great, but they usually burned out in a week and never survived storage during the off season without breaking. The entire string then needed to be replaced the next time Christmas rolled around.

There was a candle in a lantern burning in each window, and the colorful lights in the garland on the railing was a welcome sight.

With each careful step we took, we got closer to the manor.

"I can't believe the search warrant didn't turn up anything." Heidi turned around so that she was walking with her back to the wind. The gusts were becoming stronger and the roads were no longer clearly visible. She used her gloved hands to adjust her thick scarf up around her ears. She'd put her blonde hair in one of those messy buns she loved so much, but that had left a lot of skin exposed. "Do you think that Oliver or Alison burned their clothes from that day or do you believe there is validity to the rain slicker theory?"

This is ridiculous. We should turn around and head home before we get stuck in town.

Leo resembled a rabbit, hopping over the mounds of snow and ice so that his paws weren't in one place too long. I wasn't surprised when he suddenly disappeared, though he might have gotten stuck in that drift. Your guess is as good as mind.

It was better that Leo had vanished into thin air. All he'd done today was complain about Heidi not treating him with the same affection as before. I made a mental note to talk to Heidi about treating Leo to an all-he-could-stand lovefest with him as the center of attention.

"Alison was wearing the same clothes after we heard Rachel scream. I'm also not sure I believe the woman would have done something so evil with her granddaughter in the same house, either." I held up the black leather gloves to prove my point. "I still say it could be Neal Edlyn. He ended up with Ben Stanway's job. I'm just glad that David ended up coming clean with the police about his concerns. This will allow Liam and Detective Swanson to come up with some new leads."

I waited for Leo to poke his head back into the conversation and say something to the effect that I was just happy I'd gotten to spend some time with Liam. We'd finally reached the inn, though.

Leo was nowhere in sight. He had definitely bailed out for some warmer digs.

"This place is creepier than the wax museum. I'm pretty sure we just stepped back about fifty years." Heidi's voice was muffled, because she'd finally turned around on her boots so that she could walk up the short sidewalk to the steps of the inn. She came to an abrupt stop. "Raven, I'm sorry about last night."

Heidi and I hadn't discussed my gift since early this morning. The only rule I continued to stress over and over was that she couldn't tell anyone. *Anyone.* Ever.

I didn't even want Heidi mentioning witchcraft to my mother, because I wasn't ready for the hysterical reaction I would surely be on the receiving end of should she discover that Heidi had been brought into the inner circle.

"We can talk about this at home," I suggested, not wanting to do this outside in the middle of a blizzard. My toes had gone numb somewhere between Brook Cove and Lake Drive. Unfortunately, Heidi remained standing on the bottom step of the inn. "Heidi, it's okay. Trust me, I'm still adjusting to this lifestyle, too. We spent most of the day doing inventory for the sole purpose of spending the weekend together at the house. Let's just stick to that plan."

"I reacted poorly, though. I've been thinking about how I would be if the situations were reversed. You wouldn't have batted an eyelash, told me that everything was going to be okay, and that nothing would get in the way of our friendship."

I was still on the sidewalk, and Heidi had shifted so that we could hear one another over the wind. What she didn't realize was that those words were what I'd needed to hear all along.

Instinctively, I reached out and pulled her down for a quick hug.

"Thank you," I whispered, finally having the sense that everything was coming together. All was right with the world. "You're my best friend, Heidi. I really, really didn't want to have to do this witchcraft thing without you as my ally."

I happened to glance up to find that the curtain on one of the windows was parted. The fabric was quickly put back into place, but not before the palm of my hand began to have that burning sensation. I slowly pulled away, thinking back to what Leo said about our brief visit being a mistake.

"Heidi, let's quickly drop these gloves off and then head home," I said cautiously, moving so that I could be by her side as we walked up the steps together. "Leo might have been right about this errand being a huge mistake."

Before Heidi could question me about the doubt that had snaked its way around my soul, the front door slowly opened. Heidi had stopped about a foot behind me, but I wasn't about to do this on my own. Hadn't we just hugged out a pact about us doing this together?

"Is that you, Raven?"

"Hi, Gertie," I greeted, breathing a sigh of relief. Another gust of wind practically knocked Heidi over, but I caught her arm just in the nick of time. "We stopped by to give Mr. Edlyn back his gloves. He'd left them at the shop earlier this week."

"Come in out of the cold." Gertie ushered both of us inside, and I couldn't help but close my eyes as the warmth of the inn enveloped me. Technically, it might have been the fact that my hand was burning hot right now. "Goodness, this storm has picked up its pace. Did you hear that we're supposed to get sixteen inches?"

Gertie shuffled backward a few steps to allow both Heidi and I to come inside the foyer. I didn't have to peer over by the fire to know that several pair of gazes had settled themselves onto us. The sweet fragrance that I'd come to expect hung in the air, welcoming us into the inn unlike the group of people who were lurking around and watching us warily.

"The weather is exactly why we can't stay long," I explained apologetically, once again holding up the black leather gloves in my hand. "The roads are becoming almost impassable, and I'd rather be home in front of my fireplace for the rest of the weekend."

"Mr. Edlyn?" Gertie called out, not that she needed to. Neal was already walking across the Oriental rug and onto the hardwood floor. He had changed out of his usual business suit for a pair of khaki pants and a sweater. "You have a visitor."

"Raven, have you changed your mind about dinner?" Neal asked with a smile. He seemed rather upbeat, considering he was supposed to have attended his boss' funeral today.

"I came to return your gloves," I explained, deciding not to answer his question outright. "You left them at the shop the other day."

"That's very kind of you. I'd wondered where they'd gotten off to." Neal held out a hand toward Heidi, who was busy unraveling her scarf. He'd already taken the gloves from me, but it was evident from his stare that he now only had eyes for Heidi. I didn't know whether to be offended or relieved that his interest had transferred from me to my best friend. He was somewhat fickle, although he did have an eye for the ladies. "I'm Neal Edlyn. You are?"

"Heidi. It's a pleasure to meet you, Mr. Edlyn."

"Please call me Neal."

Heidi was prevented from answering when the door behind us began to open without warning. We had no choice but to step farther inside, shuffling Gertie out of the way. I instinctively put my hand on her elbow so that she didn't teeter on that cane of hers.

"Heidi!" Detective Swanson appeared in the doorway with a swirl of large snowflakes. He kicked his dress shoes against the rug outside before stepping into the foyer. "What are you doing here? Is everything alright?"

I couldn't help but notice that Neal's smile began to slip as Heidi's attention became focused on the younger and very handsome detective. This was Neal's second strike, though I did wonder if perhaps it was his third or fourth of the day. David had mentioned Neal's interest in Rachel, who evidently had turned his advances down flat. Who knew how many others there were?

What was Jack doing here, anyway?

The search warrant had been served on the wax museum, and nothing had turned up of interest. Well, if you discounted the fact that one of the older wax figures from storage had gone missing years ago. That had nothing to do with the case, though. The only reason we'd even heard about the details was because Heidi and I had taken time to grab a bite to eat at the diner. Those patrons had been a wealth of information.

"Yes, everything is fine," Heidi replied with a smile, tucking her scarf in closer to her neck. I probably looked a mess after having walked three blocks from the tea shop, but Heidi could have stepped off the page of a skier's magazine. She even had one of the knitted bands around her head so that her blonde hair was still fashionably noticeable on top in a cute, messy, haphazard way. "We stopped by so that Raven could give Neal the gloves he'd left at the shop."

"Detective," Neal greeted, though his tone wasn't very welcoming. He slapped his gloves against his other palm as he regarded the other man. "What can we do for you?"

"I'm not here about the investigation," Jack said, his interested gaze still on Heidi. I was pretty sure I heard someone mutter *that's not a huge surprise* underneath his or her breath from somewhere near the couches. "They've closed off the highway out of town, so I was hoping to get a room until the storm passes."

Heidi's smile seemed to widen, and I tried not to roll my eyes.

Was this how Leo felt every time I spoke with Liam?

Yes.

I startled and immediately began looking around, but Leo was thankfully nowhere visible. He picked a fine time to make another appearance, though.

"Are you alright, dear?" Gertie asked, her keen gaze studying me very intently. For someone so old, she certainly didn't miss a single thing.

"Of course." I gave the best reassuring smile I could while inching closer to Heidi. "We really should be going now. The roads are only going to get worse."

As if I'd angered Mother Nature with my observation, the unexpected sound of glass breaking somewhere upstairs resounded through the house. The shattering noise was followed closely by a thud that practically shook the house. Even I didn't have to be told that a tree had most likely lost one of its branches.

Oh, this isn't good.

I still couldn't locate Leo, but I had reluctantly accepted that Heidi and I couldn't leave quite yet. We needed to see if Gertie needed help cleaning whatever mess was upstairs.

"Oh, dear!" Gertie exclaimed, her attention now on the staircase. She was probably wondering how she was going to get upstairs before tomorrow morning, and I couldn't stand the expression of concern that had settled into her weathered forehead. "That didn't sound good. I should go call Rye before he gets too busy."

"I can do that for you, Gertie." Kimmie had materialized from the kitchen with a dishtowel in her hand. She regarded the detective with interest as she pulled out her cell phone. "I'll see if Rye can come over right now."

I'd never heard of someone named Rye before, but I doubted that he'd be able to come soon enough before either the hallway or a bedroom was full of snow. I was also curious as to why Kimmie was here, when her duties usually involved breakfast.

Maybe Beverly had the day off.

"We'll check out the damage." Jack looked pointedly at Neal, as well as David. He was sitting on one of the couches next to Rachel, which wasn't a surprise. "Gentlemen, we should do so while the young lady makes that call. We can provide whatever immediate assistance is needed."

Oh, it's bad. They'll need a saw to get that branch out.

My gaze swung toward the staircase, but I still couldn't see Leo anywhere that would draw attention toward him.

I breathed a sigh of relief when Jack took the lead on the broken window issue. It meant we didn't have to stay. It didn't help that there was something wrong with the palm of my hand, and it was making me a bit antsy.

Okay, a lot antsy.

The warmth usually faded in and out, but it had remained constant since we'd stepped through the door of the inn.

"We'll make some coffee," Heidi called out, surprising me with her offer. She must have seen me shoot her a stunned glance, but she'd taken it the wrong way. "I mean tea. Be careful!"

Be careful?

"Be careful?" I whispered harshly in echo with Leo, obviously not the only one thinking Heidi's behavior was odd. She'd only broken up with Patrick a little bit ago, and now she wanted to make another man a cup of tea? I took a step away from Gertie so that the older woman wouldn't overhear me. "Heidi, what are you doing? We need to get going. Now."

"We can't just leave. All hands on deck, and all that jazz. It would be rude to go now." Heidi began unraveling the scarf around her neck and unzipping the front of her jacket as if I wasn't about to have a full-on anxiety attack. "Gertie and Kimmie, why don't we help you make a tray of beverages while Jack sees to the window? I hope it wasn't as bad as it sounded."

Gertie began explaining that there was already a dessert tray left out for the guests, courtesy of Beverly. Kimmie had packed an overnight bag this afternoon after hearing that the blizzard was arriving early. The three of them walked away side by side as if they'd been best friends for years.

What is happening? This is like an episode from "The Twilight Zone".

I could relate to Leo's astonishment, but Heidi's interest in the good detective shouldn't really surprise me. She'd been really excited about running into him before she'd arrived at the house last night.

Well, before I told her that I was a witch and all.

I sighed in disappointment that we were staying a bit longer, wishing we were safe and sound back at my place. It didn't take me long to remove my winter apparel, hanging them on a hook next to Heidi's things in the foyer.

In all honesty, this old house set me on edge. It more than likely had something to do with the fact that a man had been stabbed to death upstairs. I'd rather be home drinking wine and casting spells to solve the murder so that we could all move on with our lives.

"I saw David talking with Sheriff Drake earlier. Do you know what that was about?" Rachel asked with an intent curiosity when I'd joined the two women in front of a blazing fire. I doubted that Gertie had been the one to get such a perfect inferno inside the hearth. Maybe Beverly had gotten a fire going before leaving for this evening. "David hasn't been very forth-coming with any insights."

Don't say a word. Seriously, you need to yank Heidi out of here and head home. Don't you feel the bad energy in this house?

Yes, I did sense the ominous aura that saturated the air.

I could also feel the energy becoming stronger in the palm of my hand. I began to work on my breathing exercises the way Leo had instructed me, not caring that Valerie and Rachel seemed to think I was being rude in not answering their question.

I had already figured out that the murderer was in this house, but the same old question we'd all been asking remained unanswered—who was the killer?

Chapter Fourteen

*Y*OU'VE GOT TO *be kidding me! I've only been with you for close to two months, and I think I've used up at least seven of my recently refreshed lives already. That doesn't leave me with a lot to bank on, you know.*

"It's not my fault the car won't start, Leo," I exclaimed, pacing back and forth on the Oriental rug as I concentrated on the pad of paper in my hand. Now that our evening plans had changed, it was best to use this snafu to our advantage. "Let's just make it through the night in one piece, shall we?"

That's going to be hard to do when you're going to cast a spell that could lead the murderer right to our door...and Heidi's, too. I mean, I'm beginning to think you want all of us dead.

"Heidi, these are the ingredients that I'll need." I ignored Leo's theatrics as he continued to pace up and down the comforter on the bed. We were all currently in the room we were going to be sharing, all because my vehicle had decided not to start. Nothing we did could get the engine to turn over. We were literally three quarters of a mile away from home, and we were stuck inside an old inn that was probably haunted from the days of the Civil War. "I'll also need a bowl."

It is haunted.

"It is?" Now this was something new. I wasn't ready for ghosts to be thrown into the mix. I was barely hanging on to my sanity as it was. "Will any of the spells I cast tonight…you know, call forth something we don't want to be called forth?"

Yeah. The killer. Haven't you been listening?

I sighed in acceptance that Leo was going to continue to ramble on and on about how we should be trying to get home instead of staying here at the inn. Apparently, there was an incantation that could have fixed the engine in my old Chevy. I'd gotten lectured by Leo that I'd be able to recall these spells instantly if I was a better student. It wasn't like I could take out the spell book in the middle of the street and start reciting ancient magical words that would mysteriously start a vehicle.

A thought occurred to me—I technically could have sat in the car and done so.

This was definitely a wakeup call.

I needed to change my way of thinking and begin treating these lessons as if I were going for my doctorate or something like that. I was good at memorizing things.

How hard could it be to learn thousands of spells and not mess them up or explode something into itsy bitsy splinters?

Seriously? You caught your blouse on fire, Raven. In case you hadn't noticed, we aren't having the greatest of starts.

"Are you still bringing up that tiny flame?" Dealing with Leo was sometimes beyond frustrating. "It was a minuscule ignition episode that Ted was able to put out with a dishtowel. Maybe if you'd—"

"Stop it! Just stop it. Both of you. You guys are talking about haunted houses, aren't you?" Heidi plopped herself in the paisley patterned chair that fit the décor perfectly. "I'm game for just about anything, but ghosts and demons freak me out. Don't bring them up unless they're in the room. Actually, don't bring them up at all. I don't want to know if they're in the room."

Don't upset her any more than she already is, Raven.

Leo's crooked tail twitched in irritation.

She's liable to say something to the wrong person at the wrong time and get us all killed.

"We're not going to summon any demon," I assured Heidi, wishing I was more confident in my own words. The slight tic in Leo's whiskers didn't instill any conviction to my declaration. "We're going to find out who murdered Ben Stanway so that we can put all of this behind us. Detective Swanson can make an arrest, the storm will pass, and we'll be able to get the car started so we can go home to collapse into bed until Monday morning."

I wished Liam was here to make the arrest, but being stuck in a house with a possible killer didn't have me wanting to wait a second longer than necessary.

I focused on what else was needed to achieve that goal, disregarding Heidi's careful scrutiny of the room. If I didn't see a ghost anywhere, chances were she wouldn't, either. We were safe inside the manor...for the time being.

Antique furniture only further embellished the room's beauty, but there wasn't a thing I could use to cast a spell. A china bowl had been carefully set on top of the vintage wash and basin stand. The wood had to be oak, for it matched the rest of the traditional furniture in the room.

Honestly, it was if we'd been taken back in time to the 1950s, all the way down to the lace curtains over the frostbitten window panes. Unfortunately, the china bowl was rather too large for what I needed to implement the incantation. Hence, the reason I needed a smaller bowl from the kitchen.

"Why do I say I need these things if someone sees me raiding the cupboards?" Heidi asked, staring intently at the list. Thankfully, everything I needed for the spell were kitchen ingredients. "Gertie is bound to think it's odd for me to be going through her spice cabinet, and Kimmie strikes me as already knowing more than she lets on."

Another thing, Leo continued to drone as he made another U-turn on the bed. He stopped long enough to knead the pillow, most likely to relieve his stress. *You cannot, and I repeat cannot, carry around that spell book as if it's a brochure to be stuffed away in that thing you call a purse. People who don't have your best interest at heart would love to gain possession of your family's grimoire.*

"You won't need to say anything, Heidi. I'll make sure that no one sees you enter the kitchen. I've already looked over the staircase railing. Everyone is still seated in front of the fireplace, answering Jack's questions about Ben's paranoia. Liam must have filled Jack in on David's statement." Only Ben *hadn't* been paranoid or else he wouldn't have ended up dead. "Sneak in and out, and then meet me back here in twenty minutes."

This is not a Mission Impossible *movie. We should head home. And did you even hear a single word I said about the spell book and its vulnerability?*

"Leo, we can't just leave like you can. We don't have the ability to transport ourselves out of here, and there's absolutely no way we can make it home in this storm by walking. My toes would have frostbite before even hitting the shop on the next block over." I left out that Leo could leave anytime he wanted, but he could also hear my thoughts. "Second, I'd like you to be here when I cast the spell. I'm not up to doing it myself, and you know that already."

We won't need the spell when everyone downstairs starts killing one another.

"I could definitely sense the tension in the room," I reluctantly admitted, but our concerns told me that was the reason I needed to do the spell now. Someone else was liable to get hurt, and I had the power to stop it. It was rather a euphoric feeling. "No one was happy to find out that David had broken their pact, which means we have the ability to prevent another murder."

Aren't you being just a tad bit dramatic?

"Now who's calling the kettle black?" I asked, putting my hands on my hips to make my point.

"Not that anyone cares, but you two are giving me a massive headache," Heidi whispered harshly, gripping the piece of paper in her hand as if it could fly away at a second's notice. She quickly stood from the chair and adjusted the knitted headband around her blonde hair. "I'm going downstairs. Do I look alright?"

Stunning. Do you think she'll ever forget that I'm not an actual housecat? She gave me the best head scratches when our relationship was in its infancy.

I rolled my eyes and all but shoved Heidi toward the door while ignoring Leo.

"You could be dressed in a burlap sack, and Jack would still find you the most beautiful woman in Connecticut," I replied wryly, following close behind. I made sure the door was shut tight, hoping that Leo was distracted enough not to eavesdrop on our conversation. "Heidi, you need to start paying attention to Leo. You're making him think you hate him, and he's getting a complex. I mean, a very bad complex that only you can fix. The last thing I need is for Leo to be heartbroken over your lack of attention. I have enough problems on my hands as it is."

Speaking of hands, my palm began to warm the second we'd stepped out into the hallway. The crazy thing was the room with the broken window was right next to ours. Jack and the others had used a blanket to seal off the hole and to prevent further damage. It was a perfect repair, and the room had gotten quite cold while Gertie waited for her handyman to arrive. The cold draft that seeped underneath the closed door washed over us, but it did nothing to lessen the heat in my hand.

"Leo isn't just a cat, though." Heidi kept her tone low as we began to walk down the long staircase. I couldn't help but look behind us, wondering if the room that was now blocked off was the same room where Ben Stanway had been murdered. It wasn't like I'd come upstairs to confirm Rachel's announcement. We'd called Liam immediately, who in turn had called Detective Swanson. "Leo is…a familiar."

Does that mean she holds me in a higher regard?

I almost tripped, but I caught myself by placing my hand on Heidi's shoulder. A quick glance around didn't reveal Leo's whereabouts.

I can work with that.

"Leo is a magic being, but so am I. You love me, don't you?" We'd reached the bottom of the staircase, only to attract the attention of a couple of guests—mainly Rachel and Valerie. Could the two women have been in on the murder together? I wasn't sure what their motive would be, but there was no time like the present than to find out a bit more information while Heidi raided the kitchen. "Is there any more of that chocolate cake left on the dessert table?"

"Yes," Neal replied with a charming smile. He stood from the chair after carefully setting down his cup of tea. "Have a seat, Raven. I'll get you a slice."

How can you eat at a time like this?

I would have told Neal that I was closer to the buffet table currently set up in the dining room, but this allowed me to remain in sight of everyone else in the room. Heidi had feigned needing to get something out of her bag near the door, which would allow her to veer toward the kitchen if I was able to divert everyone's attention.

There was a problem, though. I didn't see Kimmie anywhere.

What's Heidi doing? Why is she over there and looking like she's about to commit a crime?

I caught movement near the dining room table. I immediately recognized the problem, and it wasn't good.

Leo's short-term memory had kicked in, and he was sitting in a very regal position near one of the legs of the table. Anyone could see him if they bothered to look his way.

Neal Edlyn was now practically a mere two feet away from Leo's location.

"Detective Swanson, I heard that the search warrant didn't find anything over at the wax museum." I tried not to cringe at the loudness of my voice. One, I wasn't a very good liar. Two, I was an even worse actress. However, it was imperative that I draw attention to myself. "May I ask why you thought something would be there to implicate Oliver or Alison Bend?"

Jack had been watching Heidi's every move, which she seemed to be reciprocating with an enticing smile. It was as if we were back in New York City during happy hour. Heidi was always catching the attention of every man in the bar. It wasn't just her looks, either. She had a heart of gold, and what she was attempting to do right this minute proved it...if only she could pull herself away from Jack long enough to see it through.

Isn't she beautiful?

I had to wonder just how much memory Leo had lost in the

last ten seconds. He'd better return to the present fast or else I'd be in big trouble.

"We received an anonymous tip that there was clothing with blood on the fabric seen in a trashcan kept in the bathroom of the wax museum," Jack replied, finally giving me his full attention. I also had everyone else's interest. It made me breathe a little less easy, but it was my turn to take one for the team. This was going to work out just fine. "I had to make a formal request to search the premises, due to Mr. Bend's reluctance to allow the police on the premises without a court-ordered search warrant. I'm from a small town myself, and I understand that the residents of Paramour Bay cherish their privacy. Unfortunately, this is a murder investigation and everyone needs to make allowances, if possible."

"Does that mean you don't believe we had anything to do with Ben's murder?" Rachel asked, sitting forward from the middle cushion on the couch and casually setting her hand on the detective's knee. It was more than obvious what she was doing, and I didn't appreciate her endeavor considering that it was clear there was an attraction between Heidi and Jack. "I don't want you to think we kept information from you on purpose. Ben was just sometimes overly dramatic, and we didn't truly believe someone was out to kill him. In all honesty, it's just been awful since I found his body. I can't sleep, I can't concentrate on work, and I'm losing weight."

I'd like to know where on her body she thought she was losing weight from, because she had to be a size zero to begin with.

"I can imagine how difficult it was for you to be the one to stumble on such a horrible crime scene." Jack patted Rachel's hand as he casually inched his knee away from her touch.

"Sheriff Drake and I are working around the clock to find out who murdered Mr. Stanway. It's only a matter of time before we apprehend the guilty party. An interesting fact I imagine I can share is that Mrs. Stanway didn't have kind words for…well, any of you."

Well, doesn't that put everyone in the target's circle? Raven, why are we here again?

"Mrs. Stanway herself isn't a very nice person," Rachel stated in a huff, squaring her shoulders as she sat back against the cushion. "Now that David has come clean about Ben's paranoia, let me tell you that it all stemmed from Natalie. She hated the long hours that Ben put in at the office, even going so far as accusing me of having an affair with her husband. I will have you know that I am not that kind of woman."

"Rachel's right," Valerie agreed, biting her lip now that she was the sole focus of the conversation. She was a shy thing, wasn't she? "I was there one afternoon when Natalie came storming into the office with one of Ben's shirts. Natalie swore that it had a lipstick stain on the collar. Ben tried to explain that it was a ketchup stain from his lunch, but then he shut the door so that the rest of us couldn't hear them arguing."

"I remember that day." Neal shook his head in commiseration as he walked in my direction with a small plate, fork, and a white cocktail napkin. "Poor guy. To be unhappy in his marriage, have a thankless job, and then be stabbed to death. It's such a pity."

"Well, as I said," Detective Swanson replied, "we'll know soon enough what the DNA turns up after the lab runs tests on those hairs we discovered on Mr. Stanway's shirt."

David and Valerie appeared almost hypnotized by Detective Swanson's words. Rachel's lips remained thin from discussing the accusations that Natalie Stanway had hurled the woman's way. As for Kimmie, she was still missing in action.

A quick glance where Leo had positioned himself revealed an empty space. He must have gotten his memory back, which was a relief. Neal would have undoubtedly seen him near the table when he'd walked past.

"Thank you so much, Neal." I took the plate from him and began to tell Gertie that it looked delicious, but I stopped myself just in time. She was nowhere to be found, either. Oh, this wasn't good. "Where are Gertie and Kimmie?"

"Gertie retired to her room," Jack replied, keenly observing Neal Edlyn as he made his way back to the empty chair where his cup of tea had most likely gotten cold. Did Jack know something about the auditor that would make him a suspect other than the fact that Neal and Ben had an argument the night before his tragic end? "There was no sense in her waiting on us hand and foot. It's more than apparent we're stuck here for the time being, and we've been given access to the kitchen. I'm aware Beverly is usually here until late evening, but she left for home before the roads became impassable. Kimmie was taking a private call in the office that last I saw."

I hadn't known there was an office, but then again, this was a rather big house. Assuming the office was on the main floor, Heidi should have been able to grab the ingredients without any problems. I guess I didn't think of how she would make it upstairs without being seen with a handful of items.

I was becoming rather concerned, because Heidi had been in the kitchen for quite a while. Had Kimmie finished her phone call early? Had Heidi been caught stealing items from the kitchen?

Leo didn't answer me, and I was left having to come up with

more conversation so no one left the room.

"Detective Swanson, were there any prints on the handle of the knife?"

There were a couple gasps that came from my audience. The unexpected question appeared to have caught everyone unaware. I had been hoping that someone would react more than others, but they had all given the same response.

What if no one here was the guilty party?

What if Oliver or Alison *had* been the ones to commit the murder?

The palm of my hand began to sweat, and it didn't help that I was standing directly in front of the roaring fire. I contemplated joining Jack and Rachel on the couch, but I didn't want to leave the spot that gave me the perfect view of the doors to the kitchen.

"Yes, there were prints." Jack regarded me closely...a little too closely. His gaze shot to where Heidi had disappeared to, and I was truly afraid he was going to seek her out. To my relief, he seemed to understand what I was trying to do in terms of rattling the individual responsible for Ben's death should they be in this very room. "We're running that trace evidence through our databases and should have—"

Without warning, the front door opened with a bang.

Multiple things happened at once.

Leo reappeared.

Oh, this is bad.

Everyone abruptly got to their feet, their rapt attention now glued to the foyer.

My palm went from warm to hot, though I was too concerned about Leo's declaration to worry about my hand.

A stranger had suddenly materialized from the swirling snow

that had found a way inside the old house, and he appeared to have a weapon of some sort in his hand.

I remember him from somewhere, Raven. That man isn't to be trusted.

Chapter Fifteen

"FOR BEING SUCH a small town, Paramour Bay certainly has a lot of young, good-looking, virile men."

Heidi fiddled with the collar of her shirt as she continued to stare at the stranger who'd just come downstairs from boarding up the guest bedroom window that had shattered from the branch. For the last thirty minutes, all that could be heard was the electric chainsaw the handyman had used in order to cut the thick branch into smaller pieces.

The distraction had offered Heidi the ability to take her collection of items upstairs without anyone noticing. The lure of those ingredients being upstairs was almost too much. I had no choice but to resist the temptation to cast the spell. I needed peace and quiet for what needed to be done, which meant waiting until the handyman left and everyone else retired for the evening.

Rye. That was the handyman's name. I'd never seen him around town. For that matter, I'd never even heard his name mentioned in the two months I'd been in Paramour Bay.

"Leo told me that Rye couldn't be trusted," I whispered back.

The warning Leo bestowed had me on edge, but so did the fact that David and Valerie had retired for the evening. It was still relatively early, the clock not even striking nine o'clock.

Granted, there wasn't much to do at the inn. The two auditors had probably decided to read or maybe take a shower before bed. Either way, their absences made me antsy.

"I'm pretty sure we should heed Leo's advice and steer clear of him."

What a novel idea.

Leo was definitely back with full mental capacity. He'd even gone back into hiding, but his two cents were actually quite valuable.

"Rye certainly is a mystery, isn't he?" Heidi gave a little wave when Jack and Rye looked their way. Kimmie had left a message for the handyman about the broken window, but his presence was quite unexpected given the state of the storm. Apparently, he lived close by and had used a snowmobile to make his way here. "Gertie seems to be very fond of him, so he can't be that bad, right?"

Heidi and I were standing next to the fireplace, giving us a view of the entire downstairs. Rachel was practically underfoot with every step Detective Swanson took since we'd spoken about the DNA evidence, and Neal was still in the chair he'd occupied earlier. He was reading what appeared to be a magazine, as if nothing unusual had occurred today.

Gertie had come out of her room after Rye's arrival. I wasn't sure where her private quarters were, only that it must be somewhere located on the main floor. She'd appeared in one of those long dressing gowns I'd only ever seen in those black and white movies, but then again, she was rather up there in age.

Listen to your intuition, Leo urged. *He's bad news.*

"Just stay away from Rye," I warned Heidi, agreeing with Leo. There was something off about the tall, lean man who kept glancing our way. He had definitely been gifted in the good looks department. His appearance basically summed up the tall, dark, and handsome phrase. There was even something a bit wild about him, keeping his hair rather long and tucked behind his ears. He didn't have that special quality that Liam had, though. I was definitely getting off track, wasn't I? "Were you able to get everything we needed for the spell?"

"Yes." Heidi frowned, telling me that something hadn't gone according to plan. "All in one place, too. There was even one of those pestles with a mortar."

Abort!

"Why?" I whispered a bit frantically, forgetting that Heidi would still believe I was talking to her.

I don't know!

"Maybe it's just an antique item to go with the décor of the kitchen?" Heidi surmised, not catching on that Leo was in one of his panic attacks. Apparently, all the stress of tonight's events was wreaking havoc with his short-term memory loss. It was coming and going at lightning speed. "You know, I'd swear I know him from somewhere."

"Really?"

Him was Rye, though I hadn't caught his last name. I didn't recognize him in the least, but that didn't mean Heidi hadn't run into the man in the city at some time or other. The fact that the kitchen of the inn had a pestle with its mortar was what had my attention.

"Goodnight, Rye," Gertie called out, closing the collar of her nightgown a little tighter around her neck when he opened the front door. "Thank you for coming out in this weather."

"Anytime, Gertie."

Rye nodded in the older woman's direction, but his gaze connected with mine.

Why?

It was almost as if he were trying to tell me something, but he was gone before I could take a step forward.

"Now that was hot," Heidi murmured, pretending to fan her face. "Two men for your taking in a town of three hundred and some people. You're rocking it, girl."

It was nice to see that my claim of being a witch hadn't fazed her for too long. Then again, having the old Heidi back soothed my soul.

She used to look at me that way. Ahhh, the good old days. Footloose and fancy free, and you stole them from me.

I would have said or thought something to ease Leo's woes over Heidi, but the surprises for this evening weren't over.

"Rachel?"

We all turned to see David walking toward Rachel with the gift he'd bought for her from my tea shop. His cheeks were flushed, and he reminded me of a little boy on the playground giving a pigtailed girl a dandelion because he liked her.

I still wasn't sure why my hand became warm around any of these people, but David didn't strike me as the killer type.

As a matter of fact, I tensed in response to how Rachel would handle the situation she'd found herself in. Would she be mean and hurt David's feelings? Or would she graciously take the gift before turning him down gently? It was evident she didn't see him in a romantic light.

At least now I understood why David had retired to his room early. He'd wanted to grab Rachel's birthday gift. Valerie was probably soaking in a bubble bath right this moment, which had me envious.

"I knew today was going to be hard on all of us when we all attended Ben's funeral. It's not how anyone sees themselves spending their birthday, but now we find ourselves stuck in this town during a blizzard." David held out the pretty gift I'd wrapped with a red bow. "Happy birthday, Rachel."

"David, this is so thoughtful." Rachel had taken the gift gently from David's hands, allowing me to breathe a little easier. "Thank you."

Do you think Heidi will like me again if I get her a gift?

I almost suggested a lottery ticket, but I wasn't sure Leo wouldn't go to that extreme given how depressed he'd become since last night. His mood swings had a rather wide range today.

"You're welcome," David replied after clearing his throat a couple of times. At least he wasn't wearing those dress shirts that were a little too snug around the neck. "Go ahead and open it. It might be useful seeing as we're not going anywhere for a while."

Well, that was stated with a rather ominous tone. I wonder if David killed Ben Stanway because of the man's infatuation with Rachel.

Everyone had gathered around the sitting area as Rachel opened her gift. I was inclined to agree with Leo. David had a tone to his voice where his words had come out almost as a warning. It set me on edge, and that was the last place I needed to be before casting an important spell.

Neal was looking up from his magazine with a frown, clearly not happy that David had scored points with Rachel. She seemed to garner everyone's attention, but then again, she was a beautiful woman.

Detective Swanson was standing next to Gertie, almost as if he were afraid to leave the older woman's side. I didn't blame him. Gertie looked tired after such a trying day, but Rachel's reaction had everyone's attention.

"Oh David, it's beautiful." Rachel looked through the assorted teas I'd put into the tea cup, her smile blossoming. Maybe she wasn't such a bad person after all. My list of suspects was narrowing. Had Detective Swanson been right to search the museum? Were Oliver and Alison to blame for Ben Stanway's death? "I wasn't looking forward to today, but I have to say I'm not that upset we got stuck here at the inn instead of..."

Rachel let her voice trail off as we all remembered where they should have been today if it hadn't been for the storm—Ben's funeral.

"Raven, dear." Gertie had ever so slowly made her way over to me, patting my arm when she was finally by my side. "Do you have everything you need upstairs?"

Don't panic. Whatever you do, don't panic.

I ignored Leo's advice. Not by choice, mind you, but because I'd frozen in place. Honestly, all I could do was stare at Gertie in horror.

How on earth had she found out that Heidi had collected the ingredients I needed for the spell?

And how was I going to get us out of this mess?

"Yes, we do," Heidi answered smoothly, interjecting herself into the conversation. "Whoever does your hospitality chores is a natural. There were even little bars of soap next to the bathtub. And I must say, those claws on the porcelain tub are exquisite!"

She's a godsend. I take back what I originally said. Actually, I'm not sure what I said about Heidi finding out you're a witch. I just know I take it all back.

"Why, thank you," Gertie gushed in happiness. "Beverly Jenkins is the one who prepares the rooms. She's been doing it for years, and she always comes up with something special every month. Those bars of soap are red and green for the holidays. I thought they added such a nice touch for the season."

It was a relief to know that Gertie had been talking about towels and soaps versus the ingredients I'd need for the spell later tonight. I'd almost said something I couldn't take back, and that would have left me with a lot of explaining to do...especially to Detective Swanson.

Speaking of which...

"If you'll excuse me for a moment," I murmured, extricating myself from between the two women. I wasn't even sure they noticed, considering they'd gotten onto the topic of decorating. Heidi might be in accounting, but she certainly had a flair for design. "Detective Swanson? May I have a word?"

What are you doing?

I'd prevented Jack from returning to his seat on the couch in front of the fireplace. David and Rachel were still talking about her gift, and Neal was casually browsing the articles in the magazine all the while pretending he wasn't irritated with the doting couple. At least, I think that's what he was doing. Either that or he was eavesdropping on everyone else's conversations.

You're not as slow on the uptake as I'd originally thought.

"You don't have to be so formal, Raven." Jack crossed his arms and gave me a pointed look. "I heard that you and Liam are going out to dinner next week. He's a good man, Raven."

I'm going to be sick now.

I fully expected to hear the hacking Leo dramatized when he pretended to have a hairball. All I could make out was the low murmurs of conversation behind me, along with the crackling of the logs. The fire added to the ambiance of the place, and it wasn't as creepy as I'd originally thought.

You wouldn't say that if you knew about—

"And Heidi is my best friend," I said with a return warning, cutting off whatever Leo was about to share with me. Jack was the one who'd brought up friends, and it seemed only fair to warn him that Heidi was special. She should be treated as such. "She's just gotten out of a relationship, and I'd hate to see her get hurt again."

"Duly noted," Jack said with a bit of a smile. I'm pretty sure I'd garnered just a bit more respect in his eyes, but I might be about to extinguish that. "Is Heidi who you needed to discuss with me?"

"Actually, it's my grandmother."

What are you doing? Go back. Go back to Heidi right this minute.

"I never had the pleasure of meeting your grandmother, but I've heard she was quite…eccentric."

"Nan dabbled in holistic herbal remedies. Her tea shop allowed her to do so, even helping the former sheriff with his arthritis." I could see from Jack's expression that he was well aware that Otis used Nan's special tea blends for his ailments. Jack didn't seem judgmental. I found that refreshing. Maybe he wasn't such a bad guy after all, which allowed me to take this conversation a step further. "As you said, people found Nan quite eccentric. Word must have gotten around to Mr. Stanway that she could almost do the impossible."

Be careful, Raven.

It was clear that Leo was back in full form, being the mentor that Nan had intended.

"I hear it's you we have to thank in regard to David stepping forward to tell us the truth about Ben Stanway believing someone was stalking him." Jack glanced over my shoulder to the group behind me, but he then mentioned something that had me believing no one in this room was the guilty party. "Liam discovered from Otis, who no doubt heard it from Ben

Stanway, that the state received a tip that Oliver Bend had been skimming off the top. I'm not talking about a couple of years ago when Otis' prank backfired. We backtracked with this current information and discovered that the call originated from the Bend residence."

It took a moment for everything to connect.

"Are you saying that Alison Bend implicated her own husband in an embezzlement scam of some sort?"

I was quite stunned at such a revelation, but that would also explain why someone would say there was evidence of the murder in the wax museum. Alison had *wanted* the police to search the museum.

But why?

"Detective?" Kimmie's soft voice came out of nowhere. She had her arms crossed around her middle and a remorseful expression written across her pretty features. "It was me who called in the tip. I didn't know you could trace the call. I thought..."

Comfort the poor girl, Leo all but demanded. *She's crying.*

Sure enough, Kimmie's eyes had filled with tears as she tried to explain why she'd made it seem that her grandfather had done something illegal. Unfortunately, she'd drawn everyone's attention in the room.

All eyes were now on us.

"And I didn't say in my message that my grandfather was a criminal," Kimmie argued, quickly wiping away a tear that had escaped. "I just mentioned that the state might want to look at the books. All I wanted was for an audit to be triggered."

"Why, Kimmie?" Jack kept his tone gentle, and I didn't have to turn around to know that his reaction to Kimmie had earned him brownie points from Heidi. "Why would you want your grandfather's books to be audited?"

Why does the detective get brownie points? Why not me? You tell Heidi that I'm the one who told you to comfort the poor girl. Me. Not that guy.

"I believe I can help clear this up," Gertie said, slowly making her way over to Kimmie to give the young girl support. "Kimmie wants to go to college in the city. The prestigious art school requires an interview. I gave Kimmie permission to tell her grandparents that she was staying with me on Sunday. Kimmie took my car into the city Sunday night, interviewed with the college first thing Monday morning, and was back here before noon. I was just trying to help her get ahead, Detective."

That would explain why Alison had been at the inn when I'd come to meet Gertie on Monday. She'd come to pick up Kimmie, having no idea that the young girl had just gotten back from New York City that morning.

I hope that trip to the city was worth it.

"Did you know that Kimmie called the state and mislead the authorities?" Jack asked Gertie. To his credit, he wasn't whipping out the handcuffs. I was pretty certain one could go to jail for calling in an erroneous tip. "You realize that this situation—"

"Gertie didn't know," Kimmie quickly exclaimed as she grabbed ahold of Gertie's free hand. "And I didn't mean for all of this to happen. I never thought someone would be murdered. Gosh, it all just blew up in my face. I only wanted my grandparents distracted enough so that I could sneak in and out of town without them realizing where I'd gone. You're not going to tell them, are you?"

All curious gazes were now trained on Jack. Would he arrest Kimmie? Her original phone call still didn't explain the tip regarding evidence being found in the wax museum. Had it been

Alison who made the second call? For what reason?

There were quite a few strings that had been left dangling.

"I think the rest of this discussion can be tabled until tomorrow."

It was clear that Jack didn't want to continue his line of questioning while every word could be heard by the guests. He hadn't answered Kimmie's question regarding whether or not her grandparents would be informed of her transgression, but it was clear he most likely didn't have a choice if it was key to the investigation.

It was also getting rather late.

"Is there anything else we can do for you this evening?" Gertie was addressing the small crowd still gathered around the fire. She continued to hold Kimmie's hand, most likely her way of assuring the young girl that everything would be fine. "Breakfast will be served between seven and nine tomorrow morning. Please come down at your convenience."

It wasn't long until Gertie retired to her room, Kimmie following closely on her heels. There must be two bedrooms tucked in the back somewhere on the main level. I was grateful that Heidi had managed to get everything we'd need to conduct the spell so as not to run into either Gertie or Kimmie in the middle of the night.

Or we can allow the good detective to do his job. I mean, it is what he's paid to do.

Everyone needed a bit of help now and then, right?

I recalled Leo once saying that witches could draw more power from being in specific areas that were beneficial to the spell. That would make the inn the perfect setting for me to cast a divination spell to solve Ben Stanway's murder.

"Are you sure about our plan?" Heidi whispered, coming to

stand next to me while Neal went back to reading his magazine. Rachel was still talking to David. Her friendship was apparently all he'd wanted. "Ask Leo if there's any chance we could summon a demon that wants to possess our souls. I saw garlic in the kitchen."

I don't remember her being this dramatic. Plus, you should really tell her that garlic is for vampires…not that they exist. Of course, they don't. That would be preposterous.

I wasn't going to tell Heidi anything. My optimistic friend was back. She was dramatic, full of energy, and fiercely loyal. There wasn't anyone else I'd want on my side.

I could think of one with a shiny badge and an unnatural love of Wyatt Earp.

This evening was wrapping up well, with Heidi and Leo both being back to their usual selves. This was it—the time to cast a spell and discover who murdered Ben Stanway. We would then be able to carefully share what evidence or suspicions we've discovered with Liam and Jack, so they could make an arrest.

I was envisioning a double date with the four of us laughing, all the while knowing that the town of Paramour Bay was safe once again from evil and its minions.

Chapter Sixteen

"SHOULDN'T WE WAIT for midnight? Isn't that the witching hour?" Heidi whispered her questions even though there wasn't anyone else in the room. She tiptoed around the altar I'd made in the middle of the Oriental rug at the end of the bed. It didn't take her long to sit cross-legged in front of me. "On second thought, let's get this over with."

Midnight is reserved for the most powerful of spells.

I didn't know that, but I didn't want to follow up with any other questions. I'd lose sight of what I was doing. With my luck, another hour would be wasted and we still wouldn't be any closer to finding out who murdered Ben Stanway.

Another thorough search of the various items in front of me revealed we finally had everything we needed arrayed on the rug. I could see why Heidi thought this peaceful ambiance was rather eerie, but it was needed for the spell I was about to cast.

The overhead light had been dimmed to just the right hue, the candles had been lit long enough for the melting wax to slowly drip down the sides, the numerous ingredients had been separated into small crystal bowls that were within easy reach, and the necessary pestle sat squarely in the middle of the altar as if on a throne.

You're starting to hyperventilate.

Leo was very observant.

My breathing had become rather labored as I considered what would happen over the next twenty to thirty minutes. I wasn't sure I was ready to see the last moments of Ben Stanway's horrible death, but I so wanted to contribute to this town like my grandmother had before me.

You could have kept the status quo. You know, Rosemary was known for her herbal remedies for many, many miles.

"Hey, you," Heidi said to Leo, snatching him up into her arms when he would have continued to pace back and forth on the tassels of the rug. Leo's right eye bulged a little more than usual as he tried to pull away, but Heidi was having none of that. She squeezed him tight the way she used to when dousing him with affection before scratching the top of his head. "I can tell you're talking to her, but we need encouragement right now— not negative vibes."

Leo's ragged fur began to smooth out and his eyes slowly closed as Heidi's tender ministration practically turned him to goo. I caught her wink before closing my eyes. She was taking my advice, and none too soon.

She does *love me. See? That Jack guy was just a passing dalliance.*

The beginning of a smile tugged my lips at the adoration in Leo's tone, but I managed to concentrate on my breathing.

In. Hold. Out.

In. Hold. Out.

My heartrate began to slow.

In. Hold. Out.

I continued focusing on my breathing until every muscle in my body was relaxed. My senses became heightened, and it was as if I could feel the heat of the candles in front of me. The air crackled as my hearing became focused not only on my breathing…but that of Heidi and Leo. The fragrance of every rich scent of the ingredients in front of me had now become distinguishable.

It was time to start.

I held out my arms and touched my thumbs to my index fingers. The heated energy in my palm began to travel through my right finger into the pad of my thumb before following the electric current through my arm, shoulders, back, and into my left shoulder where the stream of power eventually created a circled path.

Lifting my lashes, I was able to focus on the spell book in front of me. It was as if a light was being shone over the page, guiding me ever so slowly through the verbal components of the divination spell. The words began to spill from my lips as a vision began to form and the room began to fade slowly away.

"What are you doing here?" Ben Stanway asked in anger, stepping back from the door and allowing me to enter. Only I wasn't me…I was the killer. "Have you lost your mind? Someone could have seen you."

Silence.

I couldn't hear what I was saying.

I mean, I couldn't hear the killer's voice or words.

How was this going to help me solve the crime?

Ben's furious response to whatever the killer had said was obvious when he pointed a finger in my…the killer's…direction.

"Don't you dare threaten me. I've told you that it's over." Ben pointed to the door behind me, his face red with anger. "There's nothing more to say. Leave. Now."

The light glistened off the blade that suddenly appeared in my peripheral vision. One minute it was high in the air and then…

Ben couldn't back away fast enough, but I did manage to hear the last word he uttered.

"Natalie!"

It was as if the strongest tide in the ocean had gotten ahold of my body, ripping me from the scene of the crime. I was helpless as I was hurtled back to the present, a headache unlike any other throbbing in my temples. My arms fell as my shoulders slumped forward in exhaustion.

"Raven!"

Heidi was calling my name, but I couldn't answer her quite yet.

What I'd seen in my vision had become like a memory to me...and it was all too real.

You might end up making a fine little witch, Raven Marigold.

Amazingly, Leo sounded quite proud of my accomplishment. I was too busy sorting out the details of what had happened to Ben Stanway to relish in his compliment. I even attempted to tell Heidi that I was alright, but the sight before me stopped me in my tracks.

"...never seen anything like it!" Heidi exclaimed, her blue eyes wide with excitement. "Ingredients floated in the air, the flames danced as wind came out of nowhere, and it was as if you were surrounded by a mist. It was absolutely incredible! I should have recorded it on my phone for you to see."

"I feel nauseous," I mumbled, unable to celebrate with Heidi. Besides, I wasn't even sure I had enough information to...the memory slammed into me once more. *Yes!* "I know who killed Ben Stanway!"

Little by little, I began to come to my senses. I patted my arms and stomach, just to ensure that I was back in the present. I sighed in relief when I confirmed I was myself and that nothing had changed here in the present.

"Who?" Heidi must have put Leo back down after I'd begun the spell, because he was sitting next to her with his tail wrapped around himself in contentment. He could have slightly been more helpful then giving me a compliment, but I cut him some slack. I understood what infatuation could do to a person, and I wouldn't take this moment away from him. "And how are we supposed to tell Jack without revealing your gift?"

Heidi referred to my lineage as a gift. It was the sweetest thing she'd ever said to me.

I quickly got to my feet. The spell book, candles, and all the various items I'd needed to find answers were still in the middle of the Oriental rug, but I would have to clean everything up later.

Right now, I needed to seek out Detective Jack Swanson.

"I'll just say I remembered something important from that day." I had no idea what that something was, but I would figure it out when I located Jack. "Do you remember what room he is in?"

Heidi lifted one eyebrow in response to my foolish question, her blue eyes sparking in mischief. Of course, she'd paid attention to what bedroom Jack had been given.

We both headed for the door when Leo's question stopped me in my tracks, Heidi following suit. She turned the dial on the light switch so that the overhead bulb brightened the room. Unfortunately, it did little to illuminate my mood nor improve my headache.

Why is the nutmeg still in its bowl?

"What's Leo saying?" Heidi asked worriedly, her hand still wrapped around the doorknob.

Oh, this wasn't good.

My stomach sank as if I'd swallowed a boulder.

"I left out the nutmeg."

"You left out the nutmeg?" Heidi frantically looked back and forth between me and Leo, as if one of us would be able to quell her fears. "What does that even mean?"

"I don't know," I replied, wishing I could have reassured her that everything was going to be okay. At least nothing had exploded or burst into flames. That was a good sign, right? "Leo, how important was the nutmeg?"

I was well aware of the consequences when an ingredient was left out or added to a spell. There were usually effects that were beyond my control, such as when Leo's tail went numb because I'd left out a pinch of guggul.

The nutmeg protected you from others in the vision you just recalled from Ben Stanway's memory.

"What does that even mean?"

Leaving out the nutmeg caused a connection between you and the killer, Raven. She knows who you are, and she's here to stop you from going to the police with what you know.

As if Leo's reply wasn't enough, the lights began to flicker in response.

To make matters worse, the doorknob was practically yanked from Heidi's hand. She instantly stepped back in fright, grabbing my arm. It didn't help the situation that it was as if a hot knife had pierced the palm of my hand.

Someone was entering our room, and I didn't have to wonder the identity of such person. I knew without a doubt it was the woman responsible for killing Ben Stanway—his wife.

He'd called out her name in fear right before he'd been stabbed to death.

Natalie Stanway had murdered her husband, but how could she be here at the inn when she was supposed to be in the city where the storm should have kept her at bay?

The door opened at the same time the room descended into darkness. We had the storm to thank for the brief cloak of shadows. Unfortunately, we were still trapped in a room without any way to escape.

I'm experiencing déjà vu. Raven, are we in trouble?

Leo's short-term memory loss was definitely triggered by stress. I'm sure it was something we could work on, if we ever managed to get out of this situation alive.

Run! Hide! Protect Heidi!

"Raven?" Heidi whispered my name as if I could make all of this disappear. Unfortunately, I had yet to obtain that type of power. "Do something!"

Chapter Seventeen

*C*LICK.

The door to our room closed with the faintest sounds, but the frightening noise still managed to reverberate in my ears like a gunshot. The killer had stepped inside, closing us in from the outside world. I tightened my grip on Heidi's hand as I held my breath, waiting for my eyes to adjust to the hue of the sudden darkness with only the candlelight behind me to illuminate the space.

I was about to release a bloodcurdling scream from my throat when I was brought up short by my recognition of our visitor.

"Valerie?"

What was Valerie Jacoba doing in my room?

She's the killer!

Leo made the declaration before he disappeared in the blink of an eye. I wasn't even sure that Valerie had noticed his presence.

Valerie.

I couldn't bring myself to believe that she was the killer after the vision I'd just replayed from the past. I had fully expected to see Natalie Stanway. Valerie's presence made no sense whatsoever.

"Valerie, what are you doing here?"

I released Heidi's hand now that I believed were safe. Leo

had to be wrong. Valerie didn't come across as a cold-blooded killer. She was reserved, even kind of shy. It wasn't in her nature to be confrontational or hostile. Then again, my sense of security didn't explain why my palm was burning as if I was holding my hand directly over an open flame.

"You know that I killed Ben." Valerie took a step closer to us, causing both Heidi and I to take a step back in unison. Our clothes were awfully close to the flames of the small candles behind us, but that was the least of our worries. "How do I know you know?"

Valerie's question was confusing, yet I understood it perfectly. We had somehow become linked when I'd cast the spell, but I'd misread the vision.

Ben hadn't been calling out his killer's name.

He'd been calling out for his wife when he realized his fate.

"Valerie, it's over. I'm not the only one who knows you killed Ben," I pointed out, needing Valerie to see that there was no way out of this situation. Heidi slapped my arm with the back of her hand after hearing my declaration. I was pretty sure she said something along the lines of *thanks a lot*, but I didn't want to take my attention off the woman in front of me. She seemed harmless, but I'd seen firsthand what she was capable of during a crime of passion. "Turn yourself in to Detective Swanson, and maybe he can cut you a deal for emotional distress."

I had no idea what Jack could and couldn't do in this situation, but it didn't matter. All I wanted was to get Valerie out of this bedroom. I'd witnessed what she could do when backed into a corner. I wasn't ready to leave this world yet.

Valerie took another menacing step closer, causing Heidi to push me to the side of the makeshift altar. The peculiar items caught the woman's attention.

How was I going to explain this without giving away my secret?

"What *are* you two?"

The way Valerie whispered the question told me that there was no reasoning with her. Whatever the spell had done to her mind, she'd become aware that somehow the process wasn't natural.

The unnerving display only confirmed her suspicions.

There were two ways this could go, and neither were acceptable.

Valerie was either going to run out of the room screaming that I was a witch, or she was going to try and kill us both in a rage like she did Ben Stanway.

"Valerie, why did you kill Ben?"

"I don't think now is the time to have that conversation," Heidi whispered, pulling my arm so that we could take another step backward. "In case you didn't notice, she's carrying a very large kitchen knife."

I had noticed the eight-inch blade in Valerie's hand, but I was doing my best not to panic. That wasn't as easy as it seemed. Would she attack us if we screamed? Or would she run out the door? I couldn't bring myself to take the chance.

"If I couldn't have Ben, no one could," Valerie cried out in desperation. It was clear that she was still trying to figure out who I was and what I'd done to uncover her secret. Honestly, I wasn't sure how this would go. "You don't understand. Ben was going to go back to his wife, and I couldn't allow him to do that. We'd invested so much time and effort. He was mine. I know that he loved me. I gave my entire self to him."

This was obsession taken a bit too far, but at least her admission was stalling the inevitable…whatever that might be.

"The lipstick on the shirt that Natalie brought into the office wasn't Rachel's," I guessed, shifting so that the makeshift altar was between us and Valerie. The candlelight caught the blade of the knife, reminding me of the danger we were facing. "You let Natalie believe that Ben and Rachel were having an affair so that your involvement with him remained hidden."

"Ben broke it off with me after that. He said that was the moment when he realized he still loved his wife." Valerie's eyes glistened with tears. "It was as if he'd ripped my heart from my chest. I began following him everywhere, looking through his emails, and even searching through his things at the office to try and find a way to get him back. You can't tell anyone what I did. You can't. They'll send me to prison."

"We won't," Heidi assured her, raising an open hand as if that would pacify a woman who was cartwheeling over the edge. "We won't say anything to anyone."

It was now clear to me that Ben might have been scared of Valerie's violent behavior, but he'd been more worried of losing his job had he come clean to his superiors about having an affair with a subordinate. He'd been caught in his own trap.

"You were the one to call in a tip about bloody clothes being spotted in the wax museum." I needed to keep Valerie talking. There had to be a safe way out of this situation. "You were hoping the police would believe that Oliver or Alison killed Ben to avoid the audit."

"What *are* you?" Valerie asked harshly, clearly not hearing a word I said. It didn't matter. I'd already figured everything out. "No one was there to see me kill Ben. It's your word against mine. How can you explain this?"

"Which is why we aren't going to say anything," Heidi

vowed, nudging me with her elbow. "Right, Raven?"

Valerie's gaze suddenly connected with mine.

Heidi saying my name seemed to trigger something in Valerie's memory. She now understood the link between me and my grandmother. Ben had gone to Nan for a protection spell, and he'd come clean with some of his colleagues. That fact had no doubt gotten back to Valerie.

"You really *are* a witch. An honest to God witch."

Oh, what did I miss? That's not good. You told her that you were a witch?

Leave it to Leo to perfect his timing just so.

Valerie did something totally unexpected by lunging forward, lifting the knife in the same manner she'd done to Ben.

Many things happened all at once.

Heidi's scream registered somewhere in my mind while Leo had gone into a full-fledged panic attack. He was yelling and screaming commands, but I couldn't really understand anything he said due to the ringing in my ears.

I instinctively held up my hand to protect us, my abrupt effort causing an energy wave so strong that the door to the bedroom flew open. Valerie was then sucked backward, almost in the same manner that I had experienced within my vision. She flew through the air and out into the hallway until she crashed into the opposite wall with tremendous force, almost driving through it, eventually crumbling to the ground.

Oh, snap! Now that's how a witch uses her magic!

What had I done? I could only stare down at my hand in awe.

The flickering overhead bulb suddenly resulted in the room being bathed in light once more. The electricity had come back on, revealing Heidi standing to the side of me with a hand over her mouth in shock. Leo was showing his teeth in what I presume was some type of Cheshire grin moment.

I honestly wasn't completely sure what had just happened.

I only knew that the heat in my palm had been extinguished, and now I was left with the slightest of tingling in the pads of my fingers.

We have a problem.

As if on cue, the other guests came out of their rooms one by one expressing their curiosity to see what all the commotion had been about. It didn't surprise me to find Jack rushing over to Valerie's side, his perceptive gaze taking in the fact that a knife was still clutched in the palm of her hand.

Oh boy. We definitely had a problem now.

The makeshift altar was behind me with the candles still burning. Jack would know the second he peered into the room that I was into something odd. He might not believe it, but the evidence would be right there in front of him.

"It's okay," Heidi whispered, quickly coming to stand next to me. She was out of breath. A quick glance over my shoulder revealed she'd pulled the entire Oriental rug and its contents to the other side of the bed. It was completely out of sight. "You pushed Valerie when she came at us. It's that simple. It was self-defense."

Heidi's right, you know. Jack will believe whatever you tell him, because he wants *to believe it.*

Leo would have probably agreed with anything Heidi said at the moment. He fancied her. Therefore, she could never go wrong supporting me in his eyes. I hadn't thought of it in those terms before, but that could be a major issue down the road. Heidi could be rather spontaneous, usually landing both of us in hot water on more than a few occasions.

"Valerie came at us with a knife, Jack," Heidi exclaimed, rushing forward and not giving me a choice but to follow. "She admitted to killing Ben Stanway."

Valerie began to come to, wincing as she rubbed the back of her head. Jack had retrieved the knife and was in the process of helping the woman stand on her feet.

"Valerie!" Rachel exclaimed, tucked in between David and Neal. It didn't surprise me to see that she wore a white silk nightgown. The woman did have an affinity to the color. David was wearing a set of flannel pajamas out of the 1960s, and Neal was tightening the belt on his full-length terrycloth robe. All three of them continued to stare at Valerie in horror. "How could you do something like that?"

"It was *you* who had the affair with Ben," David said, shaking his head in disappointment. His usual red cheeks were quite pale. "You let everyone talk behind Rachel's back. How could you do that?"

It's nice to see he's upset over his boss' death.

"What in the world is going on here?" Gertie asked in a breathless tone. I'm not quite sure how the older woman had made it up the staircase, but she had Kimmie by her side as they parted the trio blocking the hallway. "Detective, what is all the commotion?"

"It appears that Ms. Jacoba was about to attack Raven and Heidi with one of your kitchen knives, as well as confessing to Mr. Stanway's murder."

"Ben loved me!" Valerie screamed at her colleagues, openly crying now that the truth had come out. "He loved me. If I couldn't have Ben, no one could."

I'm not saying I don't understand where she's coming from, but murder? Now that's pretty far off the deep end.

I held my tongue. Leo wouldn't be visible, anyway.

Jack proceeded to hold up the knife, asking Heidi to step forward and take possession of the weapon. She'd pulled her sleeve down so that her prints wouldn't get on the handle. Valerie's outburst was a good enough confession for the detective to read her the Miranda rights.

"Valerie Jacoba, you have the right to remain silent. Anything you say can and will be used against you…"

"She's a witch!" Valerie cried out, pointing a trembling finger my way. Everyone's gaze veered toward me, where I was still standing in the doorway of my room hoping to avoid such an accusation. My luck hadn't been the best, which coincided with my occasional accident-prone moments…such as forgetting the dusting of nutmeg while casting the spell. "Look behind her, and you'll see her altar! She did something to get inside of my head!"

Oh, this is it. We're going to be the downfall of witchcraft everywhere. Everyone is going to know that the supernatural exists, and we're going to be extinguished one by one.

Leo's anxiety wasn't helping me gather my wits in order to react to Valerie's accusation. Heidi came to my rescue, giving a light laugh to divert everyone's attention.

It's music to my ears.

"Valerie, that's not going to work." Heidi lifted the knife she held in between her fingers with her sweater a little bit higher to make her point. "You killed Ben Stanway, and you're going to go to prison for a very long time. You're an insane murderer. Why would anyone believe your crazy stories?"

I think my love for her grows more with each passing day.

"Gertie, may we use your office until the plows come through in the morning? I'll keep Valerie away from the rest of your guests until backup can arrive. They can then transport her to jail in order to be processed into booking." Jack had a large hand wrapped around Valerie's upper arm, but it was I who still had her undivided attention. She wasn't going to forget this moment. Fortunately, no one would believe the rantings of a lunatic killer. "Raven and Heidi, I'll need your statements first thing. We can do that tomorrow morning after you're cleaned up. Just know that I'm glad the two of you are alright."

Could the good ol' detective make it any more obvious? Besides, he's not Heidi's type. He's too rigid and uptight. Did you know that she has a thing for bad boys? She loves my longer tufts of hair and...

Leo's voice faded away as Heidi followed Jack down the hallway, most likely to hand off the weapon Valerie would have no doubt used had I not...applied my magic. My palm was cool to the touch. With each passing day, my questions regarding my lineage and my future mounted. My inquiries would have to wait for another day, though.

"Are you alright?" Neal asked with concern while the others looked on. "We heard a door bang open and then what must have been Valerie falling in the hallway."

"I'm assuming Valerie thought that since Ben had come to my grandmother for a protection spell that he might have given my grandmother her name. I didn't give her a chance to try anything." As I mentioned before, I wasn't very good at lying. I should probably stop while I was ahead, but at least my story had a spin on the truth. Valerie did come to my room because of a spell. These good people didn't need to know the exact details. "I saw the knife coming at us and pushed her away with all my might."

Once again, I was telling the truth...in a manner of speaking.

"That was quick thinking," David replied with a nod of

approval.

"Yes, it was." Neal shook his head as it was clear he was still trying to sort out tonight's events. "It's a shame, though. A lot of lives are now ruined."

"I should call my grandparents." Kimmie had inadvertently smeared her grandfather's name. She was just a young girl trying to find her way, and she'd chosen the wrong path. Deception had played a big role in this investigation. "I need to tell them the truth, and I also need to share with them what happened tonight."

"Ben's murder might have been solved, but we didn't lose just one person this week," Rachel murmured, giving Gertie a smile when the older woman tried to comfort her. "I thought Valerie was my friend, but she led people to believe I'd done some horrible things. And then she took the life of our friend."

"There's a fine line between love and obsession," Gertie replied, having more wisdom than all the people in this hallway combined. She lifted her cane and tapped it twice on the hardwood floor. "Detective Swanson has things handled for now, which means we should all try and get some rest."

Everyone turned to go with the exception of Gertie.

"I'll send Kimmie upstairs for the dishes in a few moments."

The older woman had said the words in such a matter of fact way that I nearly missed the wink she'd given me before following everyone else away from my room. Each of the other guests were trying to talk over the other about the signs they'd missed, the lies that had been told, and what the future held for Valerie. Lives had been ruined, some taken, and the majority of them changed forever.

No, there would be no rest tonight.

For me, either. Gertie had ambled off as if nothing had been said, yet this changed everything. Was this the person my mother had shared her gift with? More unanswered questions, but this specific one would definitely be asked sometime in the near future.

A part of me was now restless and confused, and yet there was a peaceful quality to the air that hadn't been there the first time I'd walked into the inn. I'd taken part in solving this mystery. I'd given back to the community I now called my own, all the while becoming stronger in my craft.

You forgot the nutmeg.

I smiled, unable to help myself as Leo pointed out the obvious.

"Yes, I did forget the nutmeg," I whispered, not wanting anyone else hear me talk as I walked back to my bedroom. Heidi would no doubt be downstairs a while longer, spending time with Jack as he watched over his prisoner. It would give me a chance to clean up the makeshift altar for when Kimmie came to collect the dishes. I'd do it in such a way that the young girl wouldn't notice anything other than a few dirty bowls we'd used for food. "But I still solved the murder, and that means I have a phone call to make."

Let me guess—the good ol' sheriff. He missed all the fun.

"No, he didn't." I walked into the bedroom and closed the door, not surprised to finally see Leo curled up at the end of the bed. "We haven't had our date yet."

I'd never heard Leo laugh before, but I was pretty sure that strangling sound coming from his body represented a chuckle.

"Hey, I can be fun," I argued, walking around the side of the bed where Heidi had all but shoved the Oriental rug with all the bowls and candles. Resting my hands on my hips, I figured it would take me at least three trips to the bathroom to empty all the bowls and stack everything on a tray. "Leo, I've come to the conclusion that if I can have the power to open a door and practically throw a person through it...I should be able to wash dishes with a wave of my hand."

You're just now figuring that out, are you? Hmmm, it looks like you have a lot of work ahead of you. Aren't you glad that you have me around to mentor you?

Chapter Eighteen

"DID YOU KNOW that you're the talk of the town?" Liam asked after the bell stopped chiming above the door to the tea shop. Did he come bearing coffee? I breathed deep, instantly recognizing the delicious aroma. My heart skipped a beat when he set the to-go cup down on the counter with a smile. "I think you deserve a reward for your part in the apprehension of an insanely jealous killer—Valerie Jacoba."

There was no one in the shop at nine-thirty on this Monday morning, though Elsie and Wilma were due to stop in after their hair appointments. The snowstorm had slowly come to an end by Saturday evening. It had been a long twenty-four hours being cooped up at the inn, but a couple of state cruisers had followed one of the plows into town and relieved Jack of his prisoner.

Heidi and I had spent an additional night until the temperature had warmed enough for my engine to turn over without the aid of magic. By Sunday afternoon, we had found ourselves back at my place and spent the rest of her visit in town going over what could and couldn't be said in front of strangers.

Leo was finally coming around to the fact that a civilian had been brought into our inner circle, though he was currently lying on his pillow in the display window giving audible grunts of sadness now that she'd returned to the city.

It's not sadness. I'm in physical pain now that Heidi's gone again. I miss her more with each passing minute. This isn't fair.

"I'm just glad that Jack was still in town when the storm hit." It was good that Heidi and I had time to get our statements in line before the following morning when Jack asked us to start from the beginning. No one was the wiser that witchcraft had been involved, with the small possible exception of Gertie. And as far as I knew, everyone continued on with their daily lives as of this morning. "The end result could have been much different had he not been there to make an arrest."

I tried to be patient, but I couldn't wait a moment longer. Yes, I'd had coffee before leaving the house. But there was something that Liam added to the dark beverage that made it ten times more delicious. The first delectable sip practically had my toes curling in happiness.

What happiness is there left in the world? It's been taken from me.

"Valerie has been booked with murder and is currently sitting in a jail cell waiting for her bail hearing. Natalie Stanway has already given two interviews this morning, and I don't doubt that she'll be in court when the judge makes his decision." Liam leaned a forearm against the counter as if he were settling in for a long talk. It appeared my morning had just gotten brighter. "As for David Laken, Neal Edlyn, and Rachel Duggan, they all left town this morning to return to the city. Kimmie's confession that she had been the one who called the state with a tip about her grandfather brought the audit to a screeching halt."

"How much trouble is Kimmie in?" I asked, feeling for the young girl who only wanted to follow her dreams. "It wasn't her intention to cause this much trouble."

"The murder of Ben Stanway has definitely overshadowed Kimmie's little stunt, but I'm sure she'll get off with a slap on the wrist seeing as Oliver won't pursue the matter. Jack will do what he can to smooth things over and—"

The bell above the door signaled that I'd gotten a customer, but I was taken aback when Ted stood there in one of his black suits. He wore a matching wool dress coat that could have easily been considered a relic of a bygone era.

"Ted, is everything okay?" I wasn't about to let go of my coffee cup, so I brought it with me when I rounded the counter. Ted hardly ever came into town on a Monday, and the temperature hadn't risen above the mid-thirties. "Did you walk here?"

How else would he get here?

"Yes." Ted stopped talking to watch as Leo stood on his pillow and arched his back. It was good to see him moving again, but I wanted to know what prompted Ted to walk a half mile in this cold weather. "The red birds needed food."

Ah, his beloved cardinals. You know that he watches them for hours.

I didn't miss the raised eyebrow Liam gave as he waited for my reply to Ted's declaration. Everyone in town seemed to know Ted, and they all accepted him as just being a bit slow. The residents of Paramour Bay had good hearts, and they cared for those who they'd deemed harmless. They never questioned his awkwardness, and no one ever said a bad thing about his lack of decorum when speaking.

It took me a moment to actually process my own thoughts.

Liam had tried to tell me last week after Ben Stanway had been murdered that the residents wouldn't cast me out just because I'd been technically involved with another murder.

He was right.

These good people accepted each other's own flaws, such as Oliver Bend and Cora Barnes. I was Rosemary Lattice Marigold's granddaughter, and therefore I belonged right here in Paramour Bay with the rest of them.

Heidi belongs here, too.

"I stopped to say hello." Ted tipped his head and gave one of his rare smiles, displaying a couple of broken teeth. I returned his smile with a heart full of love. "Enjoy your morning."

"You too, Ted."

With another ding of the bell above the door, Ted was gone.

"I should take his cue. I have to check in on the older residents around the lake to make sure they came through the storm in one piece, and maybe arrange for one or two of them to get shoveled out if someone hasn't gotten to them already." Liam sauntered over to the exit, but I could sense that he wasn't done talking. He stopped once his hand was on the glass door. "How does Wednesday, seven o'clock at my place, sound for dinner? I make a killer lasagna."

"I'll bring dessert," I replied before thinking.

Did you really just say that?

"I mean, I'll bring the apple pie." Apparently, I needed a bit more caffeine before dealing with Liam. "Or wine. I could just bring the wine."

"Apple pie sounds delicious." Liam gave me one of his infamous winks. "I'm looking forward to it, Raven."

Oh, I was definitely looking forward to it, too.

I continued to watch Liam cross the street, waving to a couple of drivers maneuvering the recently plowed roads. He considered this town and its residents his to protect, and he delegated specific cases on an as needed basis. He was confident in his own abilities to get the job done.

Two murders in the span of two months couldn't have been good for his record as sheriff, though. Otis had done his tenure as sheriff without one homicide inside the town's limits. With that said, the guilty parties had been apprehended and the residents of Paramour Bay were safe once again.

Liam was trustworthy, honest, and confident in his position as sheriff.

I know where you're going with this, and you can stop right now.

"I don't know what you're talking about." I twirled on my favorite pair of knee-high boots, walking back to my place behind the counter. I even took another sip of the delicious coffee Liam had brought me before giving Leo my full attention. All was right with the town, everything was back to normal, and I could now focus on my witchcraft. "There are times that my thoughts are my own, Leo."

Your own thoughts are what usually get you into trouble. And for the record, you cannot—I repeat—cannot tell the sheriff that you're a witch.

"First off, I take offense that you think my thoughts get me into trouble." I pulled the stool closer to the cash register, keeping my coffee close at hand. "If you remember correctly, I got us out of trouble. And I'm not telling Liam anything of the kind."

For now.

Leo didn't understand that I couldn't be alone in this world while holding back such a massive secret. Yes, Heidi was now part of our inner circle. I didn't have to hide who I was from my best friend anymore, but I also didn't want to hide my abilities from Liam. I didn't want any secrets between us.

You're not alone, Raven. You have me, Heidi, and your mother.

Leo had been licking his paw, but he'd stopped once he realized who he'd added to the list.

Oh.

"My mother doesn't count for reasons you are well aware of. She wants nothing to do with witchcraft, remember?" Speaking of my mother, I needed to call her today to find out how her date went on Saturday. "But you're right. I now have Heidi, and you have no idea what a stress reliever that is."

Leo lifted one side of his bent whiskers, almost as if he were lost in thought.

"Leo?"

Something caught my gaze outside the display window past Leo's ragged form. It was Rye, walking past the diner and the police station as he rounded the corner. Both Leo and I continued to observe the man's departure.

How odd was it for me to see the man twice in three days when I'd never seen his face before this weekend?

It's unsafe to carry around the spell book.

Leo's warning brought my focus back around. We had more important things to worry about, and it was time for this student to do her homework.

"The book has a binding spell to protect its contents," I reminded Leo, clearing a spot for the object of our discussion. Should anyone come into the shop, the book could be hidden with a swipe of my hand into the drawer below. Elsie and Wilma weren't due for another thirty minutes. There was a lot that could done in that timeframe. "I can feel myself getting stronger and stronger the more I learn. I'm ready to do this, Leo. Are you with me?"

Are you trying to scare me?

I couldn't help but laugh, because Leo was a scaredy cat in his own way. He didn't do well when facing danger, but it didn't matter. He might be Nan's familiar and my current tether to the witchcraft world, but he was just a rescue cat to everyone else.

Once again, I was reminded that the residents of Paramour Bay never treated anyone or anything with disdain…unless they were threatened first. Those who weren't nice were still treated with kindness. I was no longer worried about what others thought of Nan, my mother, or me.

The Marigolds belonged in this quaint little town, and my mother would eventually come around. Were there others like us? Were there covens full of witches close by? Were their intentions good or bad? And did Gertie really know what happened that night up in my room?

Either way, I wouldn't allow our lineage to die a slow death.

It was up to me to keep our gift alive and share it with others, and I didn't have any doubts that the place I was meant to do that in was the town of Paramour Bay.

~ THE END ~

Thank you so much for reading Bewitching Blend! There is more mischief ahead in Paramour Bay, so come back for a visit!

kennedylayne.com/enchanting-blend.html

Shenanigans are brewing up once more in Paramour Bay as USA Today Bestselling Author Kennedy Layne continues her cozy paranormal mystery series...

New Year's Eve is just a week away, and Raven Marigold knows exactly how she wants to spend the remainder of her holiday break before the glittery ball drops—solving a fifty-three-year-old murder and clearing her grandmother's reputation!

Raven doesn't have a lot of time between memorizing enchanting spells, creating magical tea blends, and finally going out on her first date in months, but she's willing to combine all three if it means eliminating the shadow of guilt that has loomed over her family's surname for over five decades.

Grab your pointy party hats, bring your mystical noisemakers, and ring in the New Year with the quirky characters of Paramour Bay!

Books by Kennedy Layne

Paramour Bay Mysteries
Magical Blend
Bewitching Blend
Enchanting Blend

Office Roulette Series
Means (Office Roulette, Book One)
Motive (Office Roulette, Book Two)
Opportunity (Office Roulette, Book Three)

Keys to Love Series
Unlocking Fear (Keys to Love, Book One)
Unlocking Secrets (Keys to Love, Book Two)
Unlocking Lies (Keys to Love, Book Three)
Unlocking Shadows (Keys to Love, Book Four)
Unlocking Darkness (Keys to Love, Book Five)

Surviving Ashes Series
Essential Beginnings (Surviving Ashes, Book One)
Hidden Ashes (Surviving Ashes, Book Two)
Buried Flames (Surviving Ashes, Book Three)
Endless Flames (Surviving Ashes, Book Four)
Rising Flames (Surviving Ashes, Book Five)

CSA Case Files Series
Captured Innocence (CSA Case Files 1)
Sinful Resurrection (CSA Case Files 2)
Renewed Faith (CSA Case Files 3)
Campaign of Desire (CSA Case Files 4)
Internal Temptation (CSA Case Files 5)

Radiant Surrender (CSA Case Files 6)
Redeem My Heart (CSA Case Files 7)
A Mission of Love (CSA Case Files 8)

RED STARR SERIES
Starr's Awakening(Red Starr, Book One)
Hearths of Fire (Red Starr, Book Two)
Targets Entangled (Red Starr, Book Three)
Igniting Passion (Red Starr, Book Four)
Untold Devotion (Red Starr, Book Five)
Fulfilling Promises (Red Starr, Book Six)
Fated Identity (Red Starr, Book Seven)
Red's Salvation (Red Starr, Book Eight)

THE SAFEGUARD SERIES
Brutal Obsession (The Safeguard Series, Book One)
Faithful Addiction (The Safeguard Series, Book Two)
Distant Illusions (The Safeguard Series, Book Three)
Casual Impressions (The Safeguard Series, Book Four)
Honest Intentions (The Safeguard Series, Book Five)
Deadly Premonitions (The Safeguard Series, Book Six)

ABOUT THE AUTHOR

First and foremost, I love life. I love that I'm a wife, mother, daughter, sister... and a writer.

I am one of the lucky women in this world who gets to do what makes them happy. As long as I have a cup of coffee (maybe two or three) and my laptop, the stories evolve themselves and I try to do them justice. I draw my inspiration from a retired Marine Master Sergeant that swept me off of my feet and has drawn me into a world that fulfills all of my deepest and darkest desires. Erotic romance, military men, intrigue, with a little bit of kinky chili pepper (his recipe), fill my head and there is nothing more satisfying than making the hero and heroine fulfill their destinies.

Thank you for having joined me on their journeys...

Email: kennedylayneauthor@gmail.com

Facebook: facebook.com/kennedy.layne.94

Twitter: twitter.com/KennedyL_Author

Website: www.kennedylayne.com

Newsletter: www.kennedylayne.com/newslettertext.html